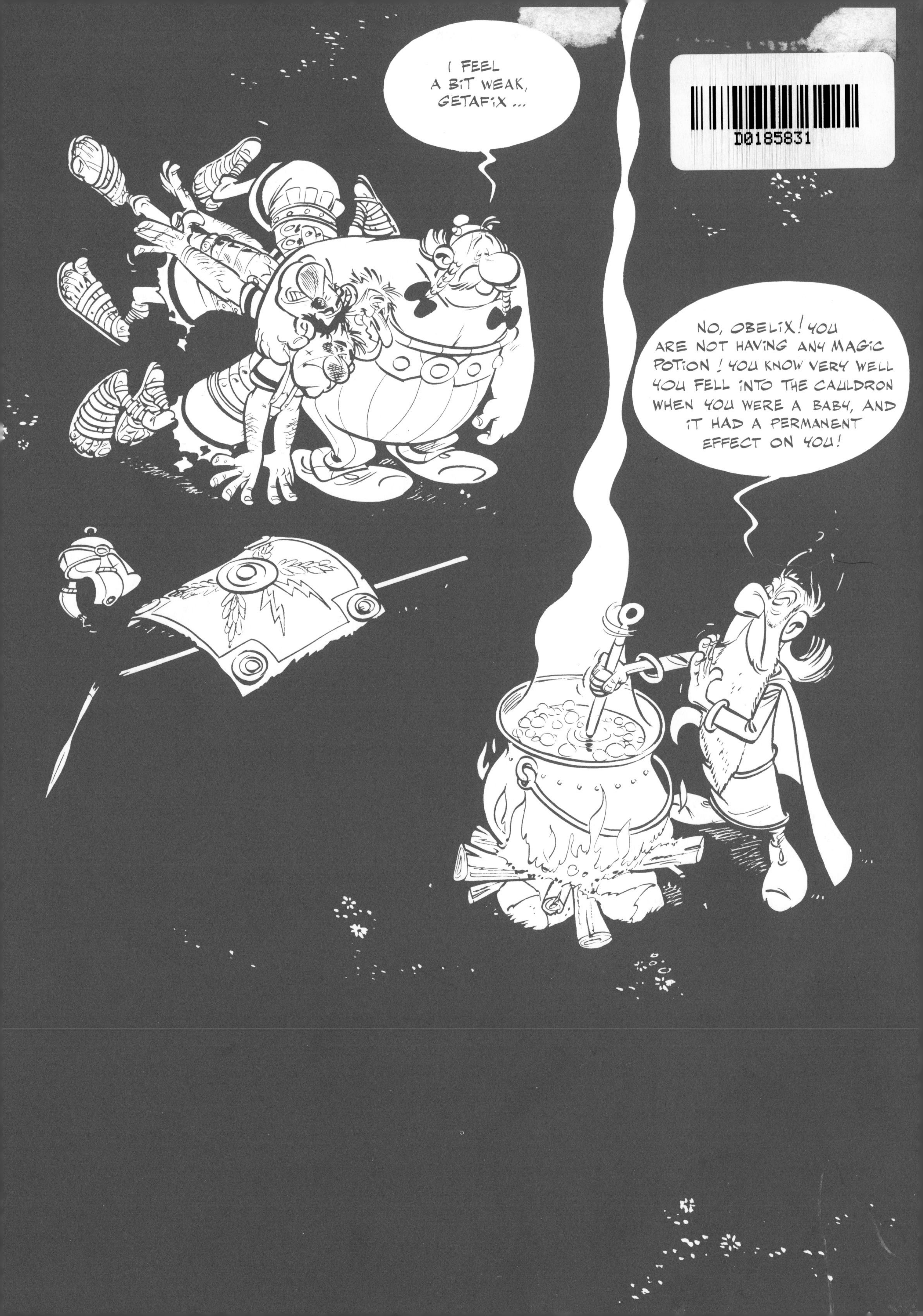
I FEEL A BIT WEAK, GETAFIX ...
NO, OBELIX! YOU ARE NOT HAVING ANY MAGIC POTION! YOU KNOW VERY WELL YOU FELL INTO THE CAULDRON WHEN YOU WERE A BABY, AND IT HAD A PERMANENT EFFECT ON YOU!

GOSCINNY AND UDERZO

PRESENT

An Asterix Adventure

ASTERIX
AND THE
MISSING SCROLL

Written by JEAN-YVES FERRI
Illustrated by DIDIER CONRAD
Translated by ANTHEA BELL

Colour by THIERRY MÉBARKI

ORION CHILDREN'S BOOKS

First published in Great Britain in 2015 by Hodder & Stoughton

1 3 5 7 9 10 8 6 4 2

ASTERIX®-OBELIX®
Original edition © 2015 Les Éditions Albert René
English translation © 2015 Les Éditions Albert René
Original title: *Le Papyrus de César*
Exclusive licensee: Hachette Children's Group
Translator: Anthea Bell
Typography: Bryony Clark

The right of Jean-Yves Ferri to be identified as the author of this work and
the right of Didier Conrad to be identified as the illustrator of this work have been
asserted by them in accordance with the Copyright, Designs and Patents Act 1988.

A CIP catalogue record for this book is available from the British Library.

ISBN 978-1-5101-0045-9 (cased)
ISBN 978-1-5101-0119-7 (Indian paperback)
ISBN 978-1-5101-0044-2 (ebook)

Printed and bound in Italy by Printer Trento S.R.L
The paper and board used in this book are from well-managed forests and other responsible sources.

Orion Children's Books
An imprint of Hachette Children's Group
Part of Hodder & Stoughton
Carmelite House, 50 Victoria Embankment
London EC4Y 0DZ
An Hachette UK Company

www.hachette.co.uk
www.asterix.com
www.hachettechildrens.co.uk

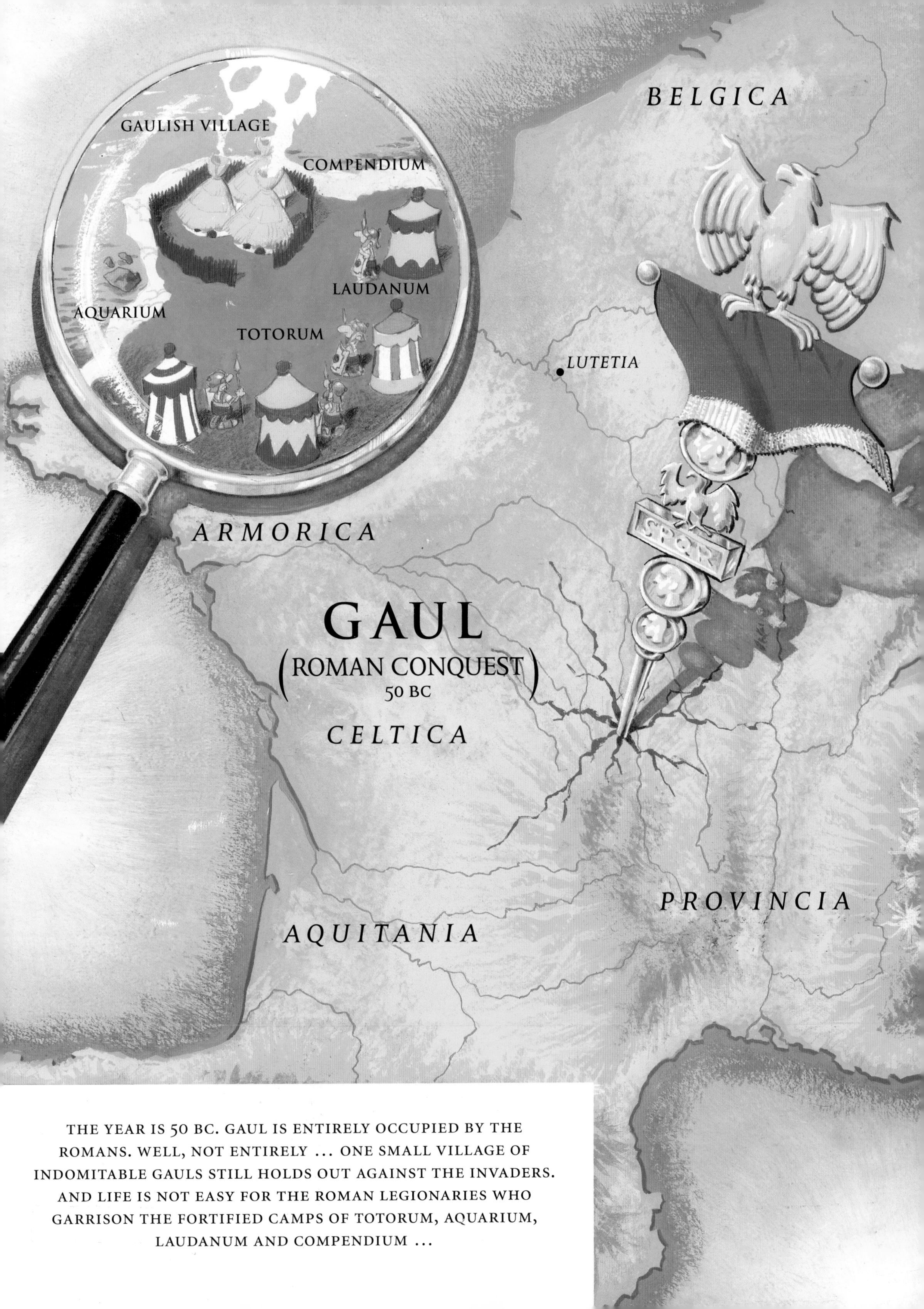
BELGICA
GAULISH VILLAGE
COMPENDIUM
LAUDANUM
AQUARIUM
TOTORUM
LUTETIA
SPQR
ARMORICA
GAUL
(ROMAN CONQUEST)
50 BC
CELTICA
PROVINCIA
AQUITANIA

THE YEAR IS 50 BC. GAUL IS ENTIRELY OCCUPIED BY THE ROMANS. WELL, NOT ENTIRELY ... ONE SMALL VILLAGE OF INDOMITABLE GAULS STILL HOLDS OUT AGAINST THE INVADERS. AND LIFE IS NOT EASY FOR THE ROMAN LEGIONARIES WHO GARRISON THE FORTIFIED CAMPS OF TOTORUM, AQUARIUM, LAUDANUM AND COMPENDIUM ...

ASTERIX, THE HERO OF THESE ADVENTURES. A SHREWD, CUNNING LITTLE WARRIOR, ALL PERILOUS MISSIONS ARE IMMEDIATELY ENTRUSTED TO HIM. ASTERIX GETS HIS SUPERHUMAN STRENGTH FROM THE MAGIC POTION BREWED BY THE DRUID GETAFIX . . .

OBELIX, ASTERIX'S INSEPARABLE FRIEND. A MENHIR DELIVERY MAN BY TRADE, ADDICTED TO WILD BOAR. OBELIX IS ALWAYS READY TO DROP EVERYTHING AND GO OFF ON A NEW ADVENTURE WITH ASTERIX — SO LONG AS THERE'S WILD BOAR TO EAT, AND PLENTY OF FIGHTING. HIS CONSTANT COMPANION IS DOGMATIX, THE ONLY KNOWN CANINE ECOLOGIST, WHO HOWLS WITH DESPAIR WHEN A TREE IS CUT DOWN.

GETAFIX, THE VENERABLE VILLAGE DRUID, GATHERS MISTLETOE AND BREWS MAGIC POTIONS. HIS SPECIALITY IS THE POTION WHICH GIVES THE DRINKER SUPERHUMAN STRENGTH. BUT GETAFIX ALSO HAS OTHER RECIPES UP HIS SLEEVE . . .

CACOFONIX, THE BARD. OPINION IS DIVIDED AS TO HIS MUSICAL GIFTS. CACOFONIX THINKS HE'S A GENIUS. EVERY-ONE ELSE THINKS HE'S UNSPEAKABLE. BUT SO LONG AS HE DOESN'T SPEAK, LET ALONE SING, EVERYBODY LIKES HIM . . .

FINALLY, VITALSTATISTIX, THE CHIEF OF THE TRIBE. MAJESTIC, BRAVE AND HOT-TEMPERED, THE OLD WARRIOR IS RESPECTED BY HIS MEN AND FEARED BY HIS ENEMIES. VITALSTATISTIX HIMSELF HAS ONLY ONE FEAR, HE IS AFRAID THE SKY MAY FALL ON HIS HEAD TOMORROW. BUT AS HE ALWAYS SAYS, TOMORROW NEVER COMES.

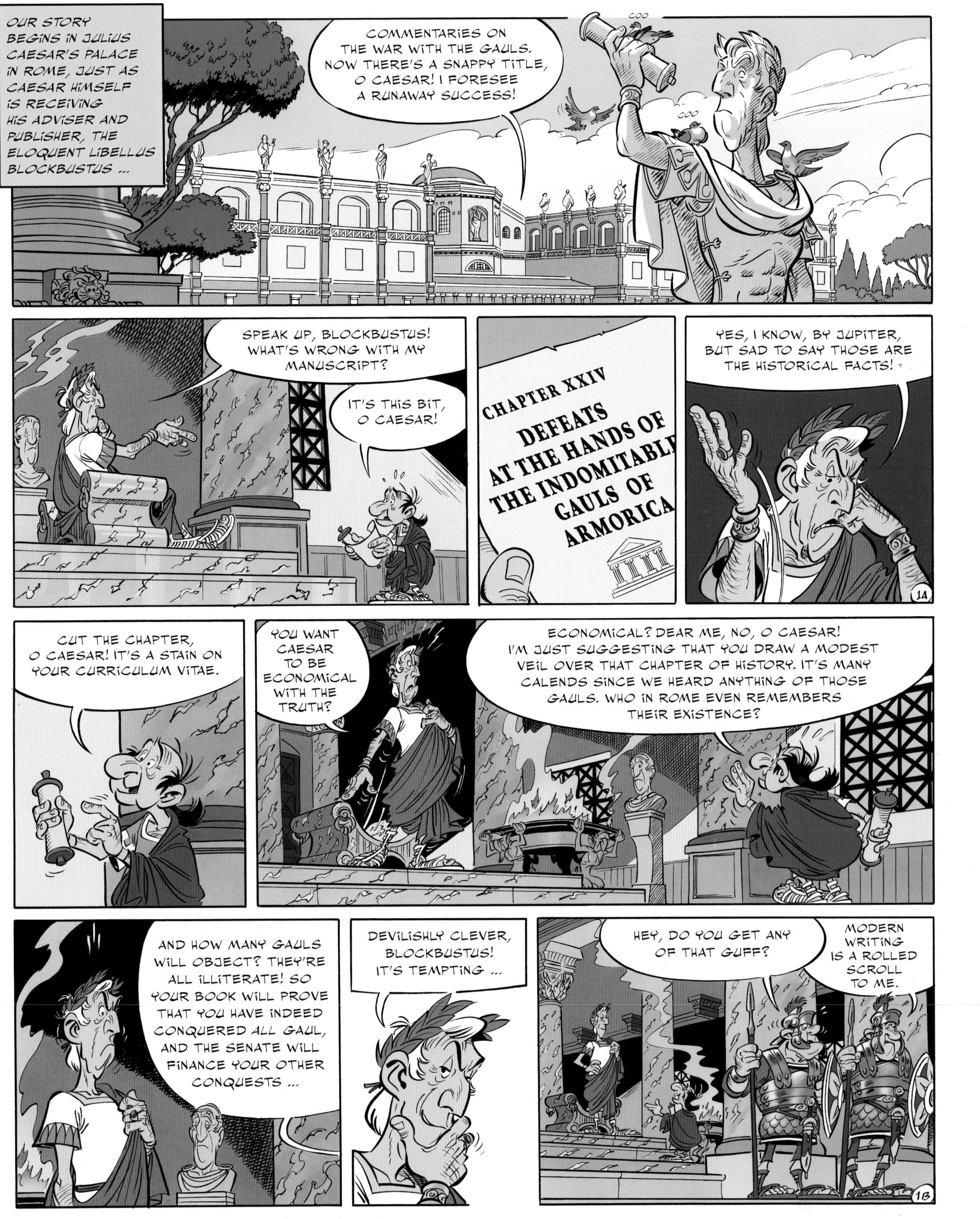
OUR STORY BEGINS IN JULIUS CAESAR'S PALACE IN ROME, JUST AS CAESAR HIMSELF IS RECEIVING HIS ADVISER AND PUBLISHER, THE ELOQUENT LIBELLUS BLOCKBUSTUS ...
COO
COMMENTARIES ON THE WAR WITH THE GAULS. NOW THERE'S A SNAPPY TITLE, O CAESAR! I FORESEE A RUNAWAY SUCCESS!
COO
SPEAK UP, BLOCKBUSTUS! WHAT'S WRONG WITH MY MANUSCRIPT?
IT'S THIS BIT, O CAESAR!
CHAPTER XXIV
DEFEATS AT THE HANDS OF THE INDOMITABLE GAULS OF ARMORICA
YES, I KNOW, BY JUPITER, BUT SAD TO SAY THOSE ARE THE HISTORICAL FACTS!
1A
CUT THE CHAPTER, O CAESAR! IT'S A STAIN ON YOUR CURRICULUM VITAE.
YOU WANT CAESAR TO BE ECONOMICAL WITH THE TRUTH?
ECONOMICAL? DEAR ME, NO, O CAESAR! I'M JUST SUGGESTING THAT YOU DRAW A MODEST VEIL OVER THAT CHAPTER OF HISTORY. IT'S MANY CALENDS SINCE WE HEARD ANYTHING OF THOSE GAULS. WHO IN ROME EVEN REMEMBERS THEIR EXISTENCE?
AND HOW MANY GAULS WILL OBJECT? THEY'RE ALL ILLITERATE! SO YOUR BOOK WILL PROVE THAT YOU HAVE INDEED CONQUERED ALL GAUL, AND THE SENATE WILL FINANCE YOUR OTHER CONQUESTS ...
DEVILISHLY CLEVER, BLOCKBUSTUS! IT'S TEMPTING ...
HEY, DO YOU GET ANY OF THAT GUFF?
MODERN WRITING IS A ROLLED SCROLL TO ME.
1B

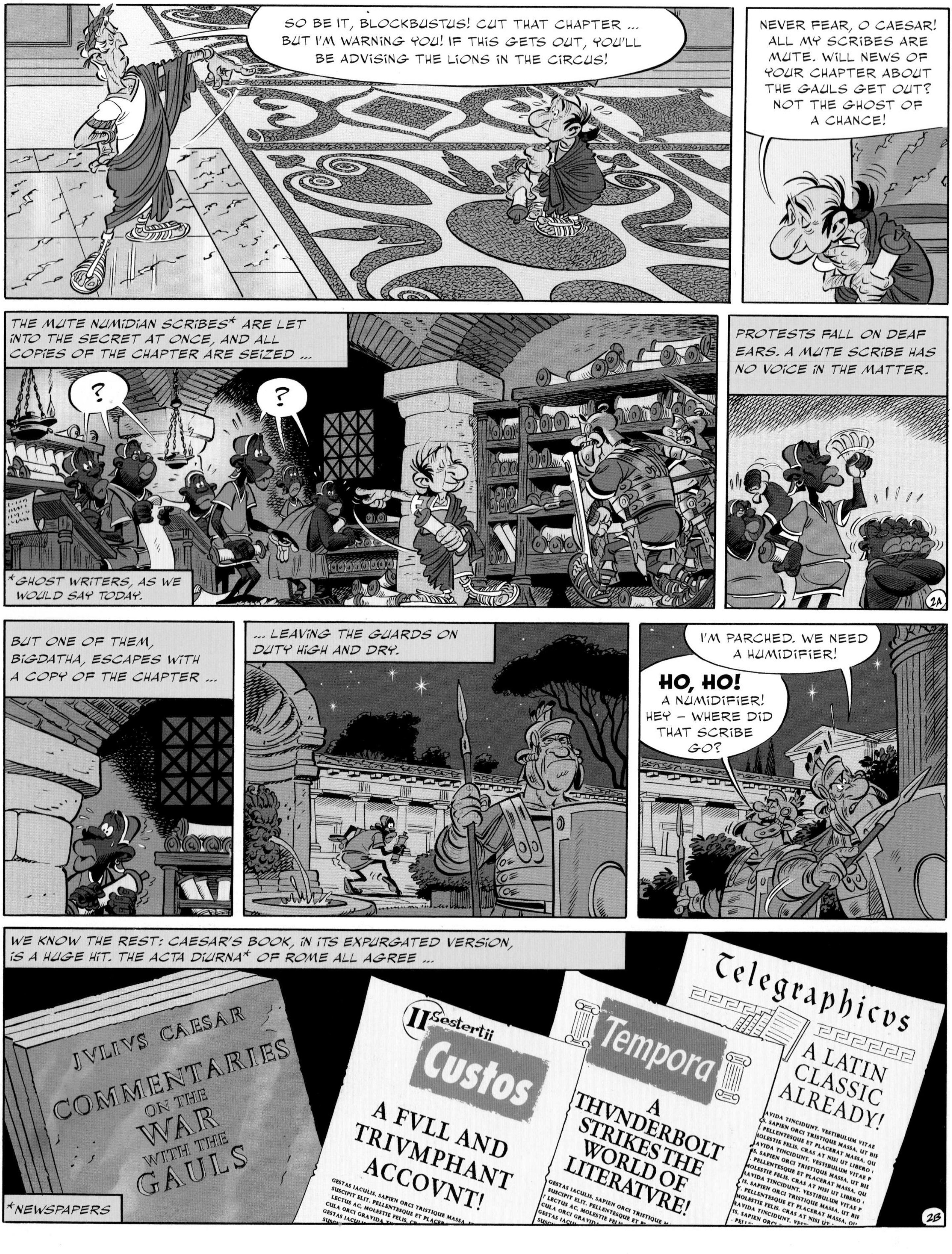
SO BE IT, BLOCKBUSTUS! CUT THAT CHAPTER ... BUT I'M WARNING YOU! IF THIS GETS OUT, YOU'LL BE ADVISING THE LIONS IN THE CIRCUS!
NEVER FEAR, O CAESAR! ALL MY SCRIBES ARE MUTE. WILL NEWS OF YOUR CHAPTER ABOUT THE GAULS GET OUT? NOT THE GHOST OF A CHANCE!
THE MUTE NUMIDIAN SCRIBES* ARE LET INTO THE SECRET AT ONCE, AND ALL COPIES OF THE CHAPTER ARE SEIZED ...
?
?
*GHOST WRITERS, AS WE WOULD SAY TODAY.
PROTESTS FALL ON DEAF EARS. A MUTE SCRIBE HAS NO VOICE IN THE MATTER.
BUT ONE OF THEM, BIGDATHA, ESCAPES WITH A COPY OF THE CHAPTER ...
... LEAVING THE GUARDS ON DUTY HIGH AND DRY.
I'M PARCHED. WE NEED A HUMIDIFIER!
HO, HO! A NUMIDIFIER! HEY – WHERE DID THAT SCRIBE GO?
WE KNOW THE REST: CAESAR'S BOOK, IN ITS EXPURGATED VERSION, IS A HUGE HIT. THE ACTA DIURNA* OF ROME ALL AGREE ...
JVLIVS CAESAR
COMMENTARIES ON THE WAR WITH THE GAULS
II Sestertii
Custos
A FVLL AND TRIVMPHANT ACCOVNT!
Tempora
A THVNDERBOLT STRIKES THE WORLD OF LITERATVRE!
Telegraphicvs
A LATIN CLASSIC ALREADY!
*NEWSPAPERS

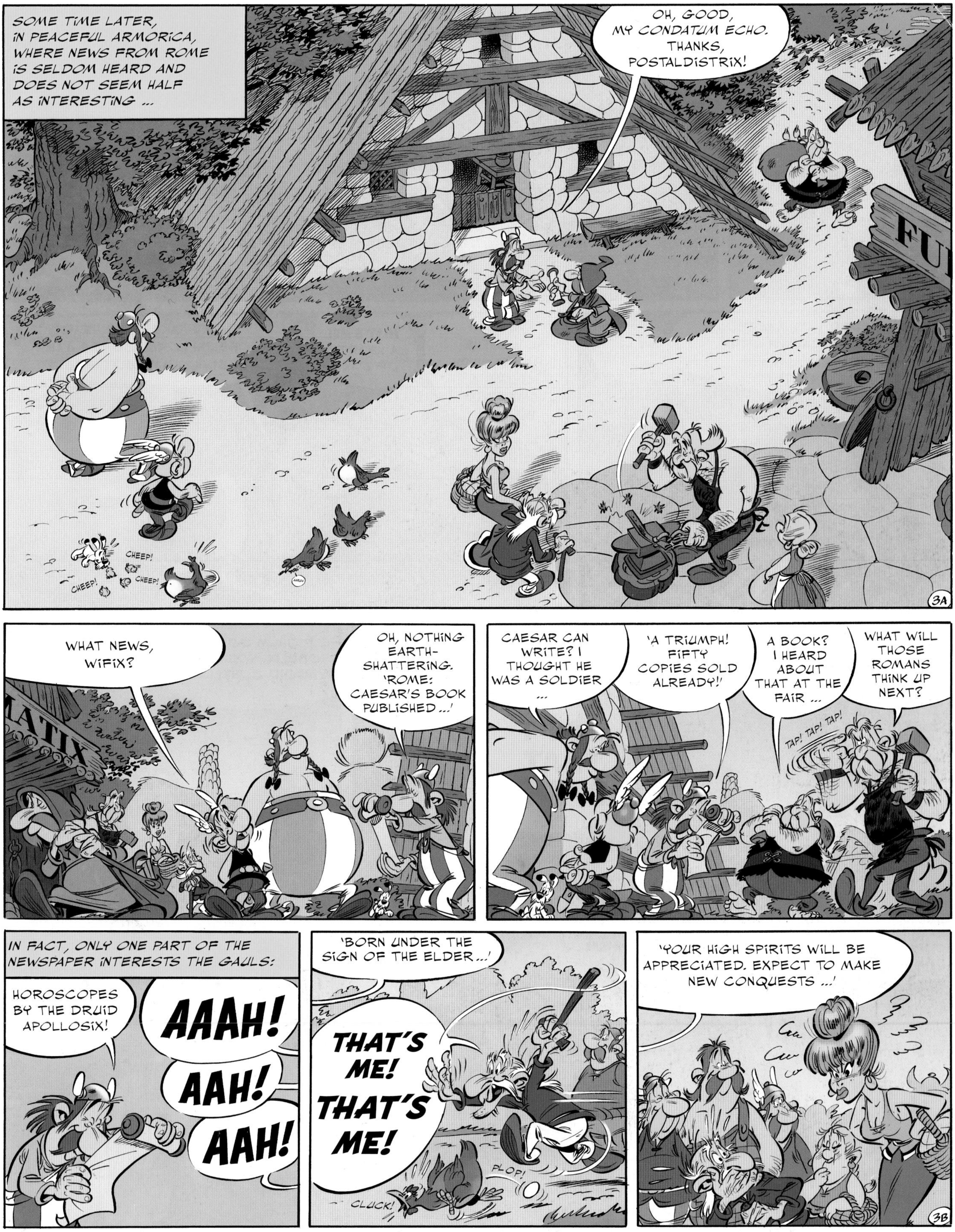
SOME TIME LATER, IN PEACEFUL ARMORICA, WHERE NEWS FROM ROME IS SELDOM HEARD AND DOES NOT SEEM HALF AS INTERESTING ...
OH, GOOD, MY CONDATUM ECHO. THANKS, POSTALDISTRIX!
CHEEP!
CHEEP!
CHEEP!
3A
WHAT NEWS, WIFIX?
OH, NOTHING EARTH-SHATTERING. 'ROME: CAESAR'S BOOK PUBLISHED ...'
CAESAR CAN WRITE? I THOUGHT HE WAS A SOLDIER ...
'A TRIUMPH! FIFTY COPIES SOLD ALREADY!'
A BOOK? I HEARD ABOUT THAT AT THE FAIR ...
WHAT WILL THOSE ROMANS THINK UP NEXT?
TAP! TAP! TAP!
IN FACT, ONLY ONE PART OF THE NEWSPAPER INTERESTS THE GAULS:
HOROSCOPES BY THE DRUID APOLLOSIX!
AAAH! AAH! AAH!
'BORN UNDER THE SIGN OF THE ELDER ...'
THAT'S ME! THAT'S ME!
PLOP!
CLUCK!
'YOUR HIGH SPIRITS WILL BE APPRECIATED. EXPECT TO MAKE NEW CONQUESTS ...'
3B

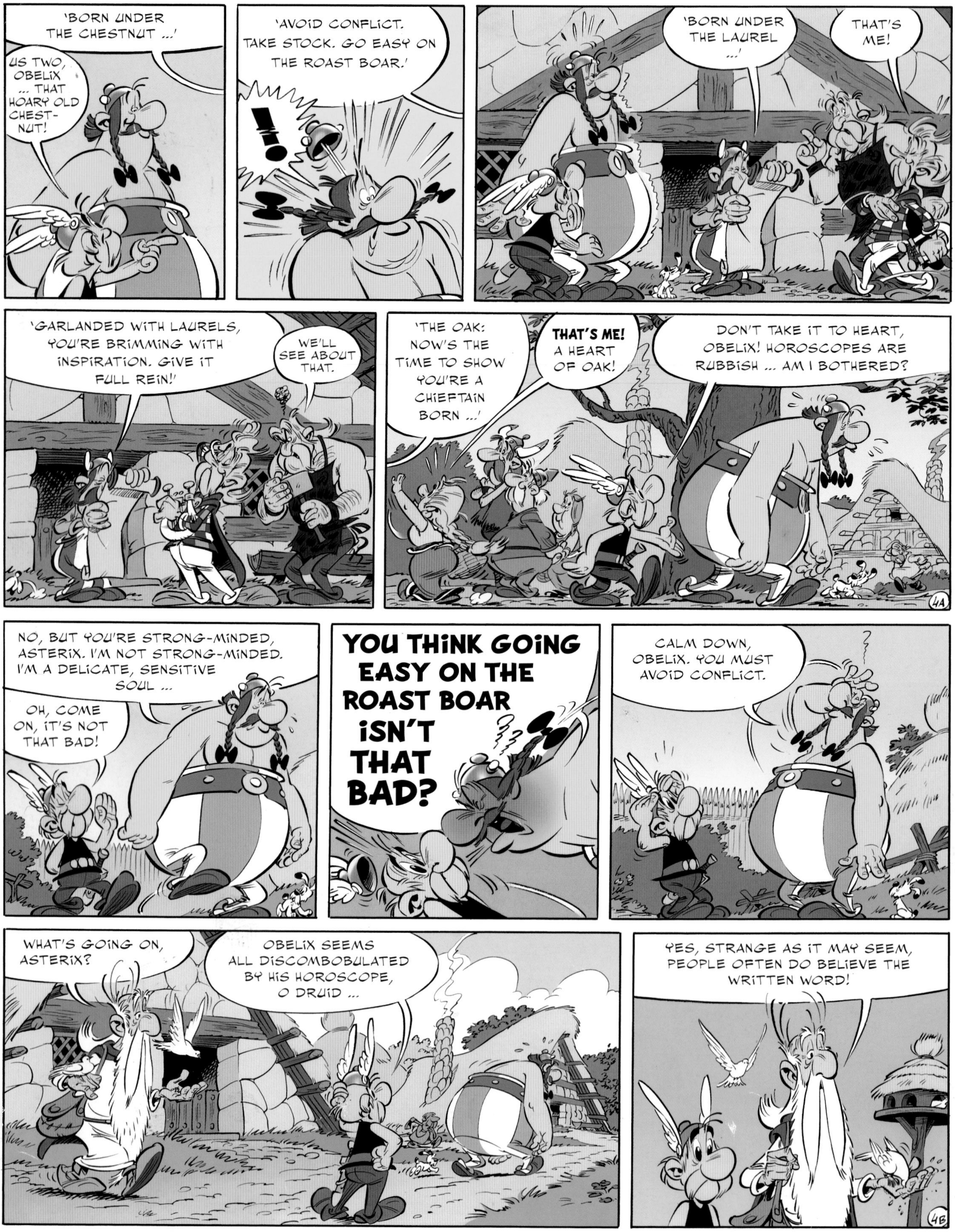
'BORN UNDER THE CHESTNUT ...'
US TWO, OBELIX ... THAT HOARY OLD CHEST-NUT!
'AVOID CONFLICT. TAKE STOCK. GO EASY ON THE ROAST BOAR.'
!!
'BORN UNDER THE LAUREL ...'
THAT'S ME!
'GARLANDED WITH LAURELS, YOU'RE BRIMMING WITH INSPIRATION. GIVE IT FULL REIN!'
WE'LL SEE ABOUT THAT.
'THE OAK: NOW'S THE TIME TO SHOW YOU'RE A CHIEFTAIN BORN ...'
THAT'S ME! A HEART OF OAK!
DON'T TAKE IT TO HEART, OBELIX! HOROSCOPES ARE RUBBISH ... AM I BOTHERED?
NO, BUT YOU'RE STRONG-MINDED, ASTERIX. I'M NOT STRONG-MINDED. I'M A DELICATE, SENSITIVE SOUL ...
OH, COME ON, IT'S NOT THAT BAD!
YOU THINK GOING EASY ON THE ROAST BOAR ISN'T THAT BAD?
CALM DOWN, OBELIX. YOU MUST AVOID CONFLICT.
WHAT'S GOING ON, ASTERIX?
OBELIX SEEMS ALL DISCOMBOBULATED BY HIS HOROSCOPE, O DRUID ...
YES, STRANGE AS IT MAY SEEM, PEOPLE OFTEN DO BELIEVE THE WRITTEN WORD!

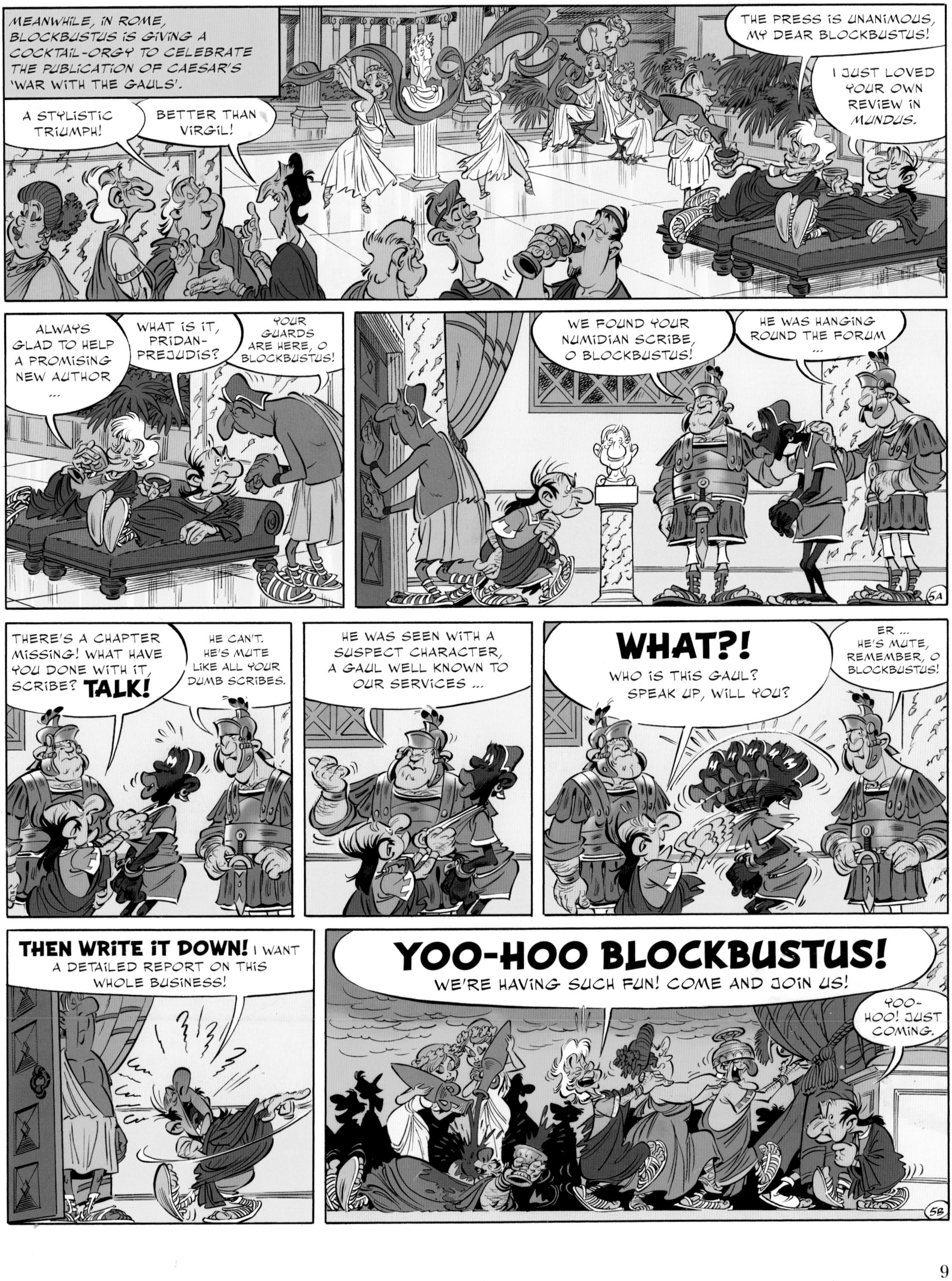
MEANWHILE, IN ROME, BLOCKBUSTUS IS GIVING A COCKTAIL-ORGY TO CELEBRATE THE PUBLICATION OF CAESAR'S 'WAR WITH THE GAULS'.
A STYLISTIC TRIUMPH!
BETTER THAN VIRGIL!
THE PRESS IS UNANIMOUS, MY DEAR BLOCKBUSTUS!
I JUST LOVED YOUR OWN REVIEW IN MUNDUS.
ALWAYS GLAD TO HELP A PROMISING NEW AUTHOR ...
WHAT IS IT, PRIDAN-PREJUDIS?
YOUR GUARDS ARE HERE, O BLOCKBUSTUS!
WE FOUND YOUR NUMIDIAN SCRIBE, O BLOCKBUSTUS!
HE WAS HANGING ROUND THE FORUM ...
5A
THERE'S A CHAPTER MISSING! WHAT HAVE YOU DONE WITH IT, SCRIBE? TALK!
HE CAN'T. HE'S MUTE LIKE ALL YOUR DUMB SCRIBES.
HE WAS SEEN WITH A SUSPECT CHARACTER, A GAUL WELL KNOWN TO OUR SERVICES ...
WHAT?! WHO IS THIS GAUL? SPEAK UP, WILL YOU?
ER ... HE'S MUTE, REMEMBER, O BLOCKBUSTUS!
THEN WRITE IT DOWN! I WANT A DETAILED REPORT ON THIS WHOLE BUSINESS!
YOO-HOO BLOCKBUSTUS! WE'RE HAVING SUCH FUN! COME AND JOIN US!
YOO-HOO! JUST COMING.
5B

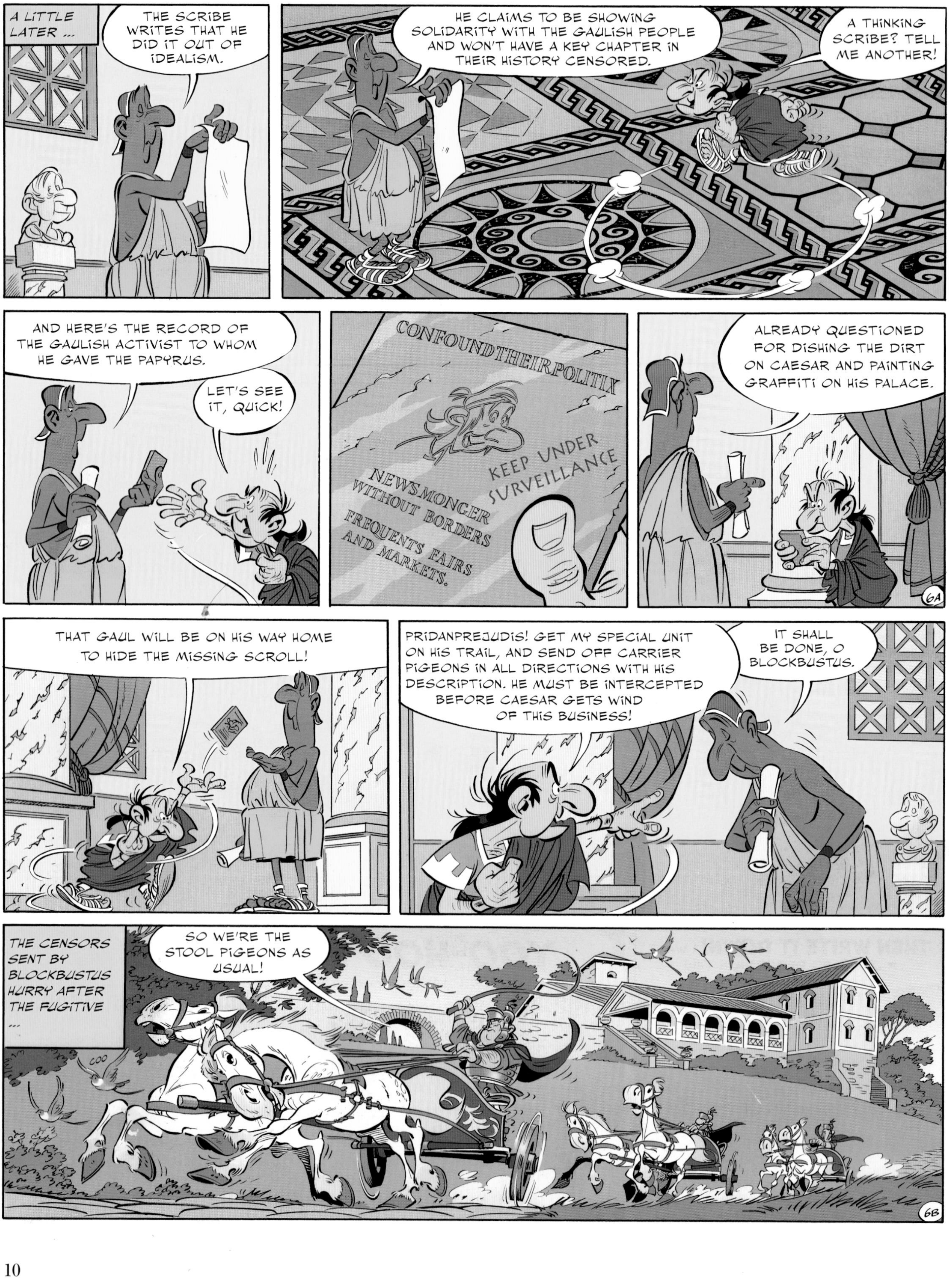
A LITTLE LATER ...
THE SCRIBE WRITES THAT HE DID IT OUT OF IDEALISM.
HE CLAIMS TO BE SHOWING SOLIDARITY WITH THE GAULISH PEOPLE AND WON'T HAVE A KEY CHAPTER IN THEIR HISTORY CENSORED.
A THINKING SCRIBE? TELL ME ANOTHER!
AND HERE'S THE RECORD OF THE GAULISH ACTIVIST TO WHOM HE GAVE THE PAPYRUS.
LET'S SEE IT, QUICK!
CONFOUNDTHEIRPOLITIX
KEEP UNDER SURVEILLANCE
NEWSMONGER WITHOUT BORDERS
FREQUENTS FAIRS AND MARKETS.
ALREADY QUESTIONED FOR DISHING THE DIRT ON CAESAR AND PAINTING GRAFFITI ON HIS PALACE.
6A
THAT GAUL WILL BE ON HIS WAY HOME TO HIDE THE MISSING SCROLL!
PRIDANPREJUDIS! GET MY SPECIAL UNIT ON HIS TRAIL, AND SEND OFF CARRIER PIGEONS IN ALL DIRECTIONS WITH HIS DESCRIPTION. HE MUST BE INTERCEPTED BEFORE CAESAR GETS WIND OF THIS BUSINESS!
IT SHALL BE DONE, O BLOCKBUSTUS.
THE CENSORS SENT BY BLOCKBUSTUS HURRY AFTER THE FUGITIVE ...
SO WE'RE THE STOOL PIGEONS AS USUAL!
COO
6B

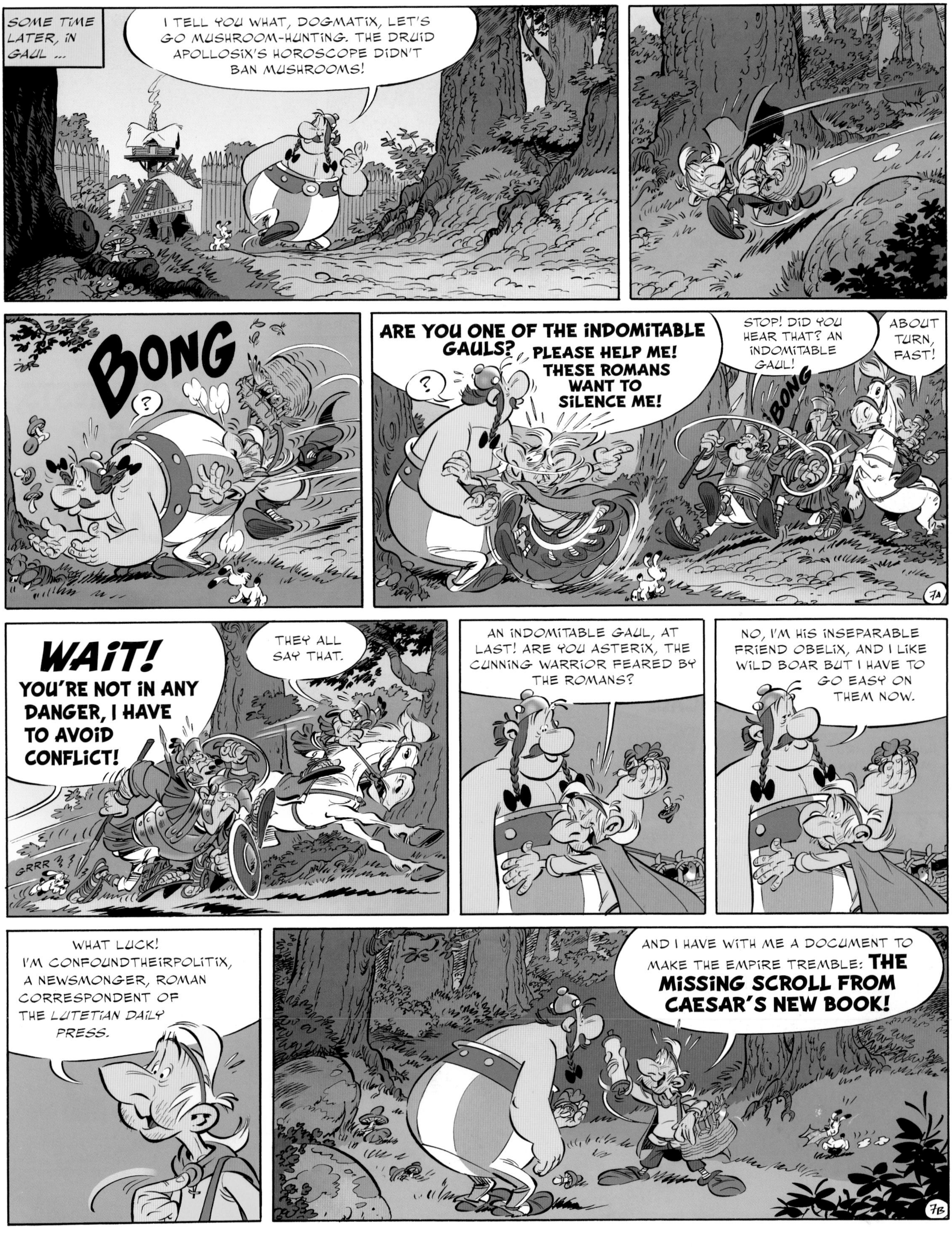
SOME TIME LATER, IN GAUL ...
I TELL YOU WHAT, DOGMATIX, LET'S GO MUSHROOM-HUNTING. THE DRUID APOLLOSIX'S HOROSCOPE DIDN'T BAN MUSHROOMS!
UNHYGIENIX
BONG
?
ARE YOU ONE OF THE INDOMITABLE GAULS? PLEASE HELP ME! THESE ROMANS WANT TO SILENCE ME!
?
STOP! DID YOU HEAR THAT? AN INDOMITABLE GAUL!
ABOUT TURN, FAST!
BONG
WAIT! YOU'RE NOT IN ANY DANGER, I HAVE TO AVOID CONFLICT!
THEY ALL SAY THAT.
GRRR
AN INDOMITABLE GAUL, AT LAST! ARE YOU ASTERIX, THE CUNNING WARRIOR FEARED BY THE ROMANS?
NO, I'M HIS INSEPARABLE FRIEND OBELIX, AND I LIKE WILD BOAR BUT I HAVE TO GO EASY ON THEM NOW.
WHAT LUCK! I'M CONFOUNDTHEIRPOLITIX, A NEWSMONGER, ROMAN CORRESPONDENT OF THE LUTETIAN DAILY PRESS.
AND I HAVE WITH ME A DOCUMENT TO MAKE THE EMPIRE TREMBLE: THE MISSING SCROLL FROM CAESAR'S NEW BOOK!

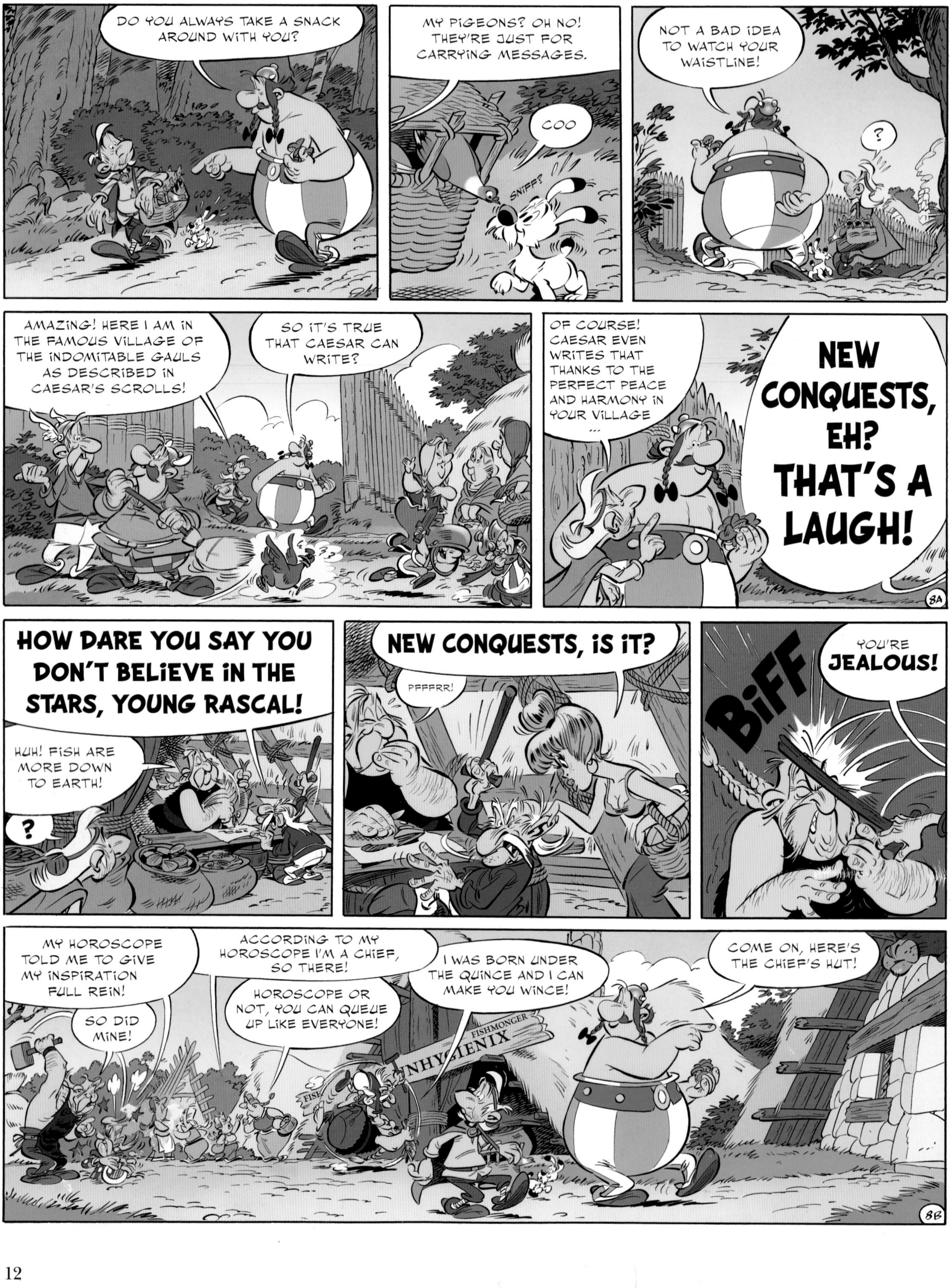
DO YOU ALWAYS TAKE A SNACK AROUND WITH YOU?
COO
MY PIGEONS? OH NO! THEY'RE JUST FOR CARRYING MESSAGES.
COO
SNIFF?
NOT A BAD IDEA TO WATCH YOUR WAISTLINE!
?
AMAZING! HERE I AM IN THE FAMOUS VILLAGE OF THE INDOMITABLE GAULS AS DESCRIBED IN CAESAR'S SCROLLS!
SO IT'S TRUE THAT CAESAR CAN WRITE?
OF COURSE! CAESAR EVEN WRITES THAT THANKS TO THE PERFECT PEACE AND HARMONY IN YOUR VILLAGE ...
NEW CONQUESTS, EH? THAT'S A LAUGH!
8A
HOW DARE YOU SAY YOU DON'T BELIEVE IN THE STARS, YOUNG RASCAL!
HUH! FISH ARE MORE DOWN TO EARTH!
?
NEW CONQUESTS, IS IT?
PFFFRR!
BIFF
YOU'RE JEALOUS!
MY HOROSCOPE TOLD ME TO GIVE MY INSPIRATION FULL REIN!
SO DID MINE!
ACCORDING TO MY HOROSCOPE I'M A CHIEF, SO THERE!
HOROSCOPE OR NOT, YOU CAN QUEUE UP LIKE EVERYONE!
I WAS BORN UNDER THE QUINCE AND I CAN MAKE YOU WINCE!
FISHMONGER
COME ON, HERE'S THE CHIEF'S HUT!
8B

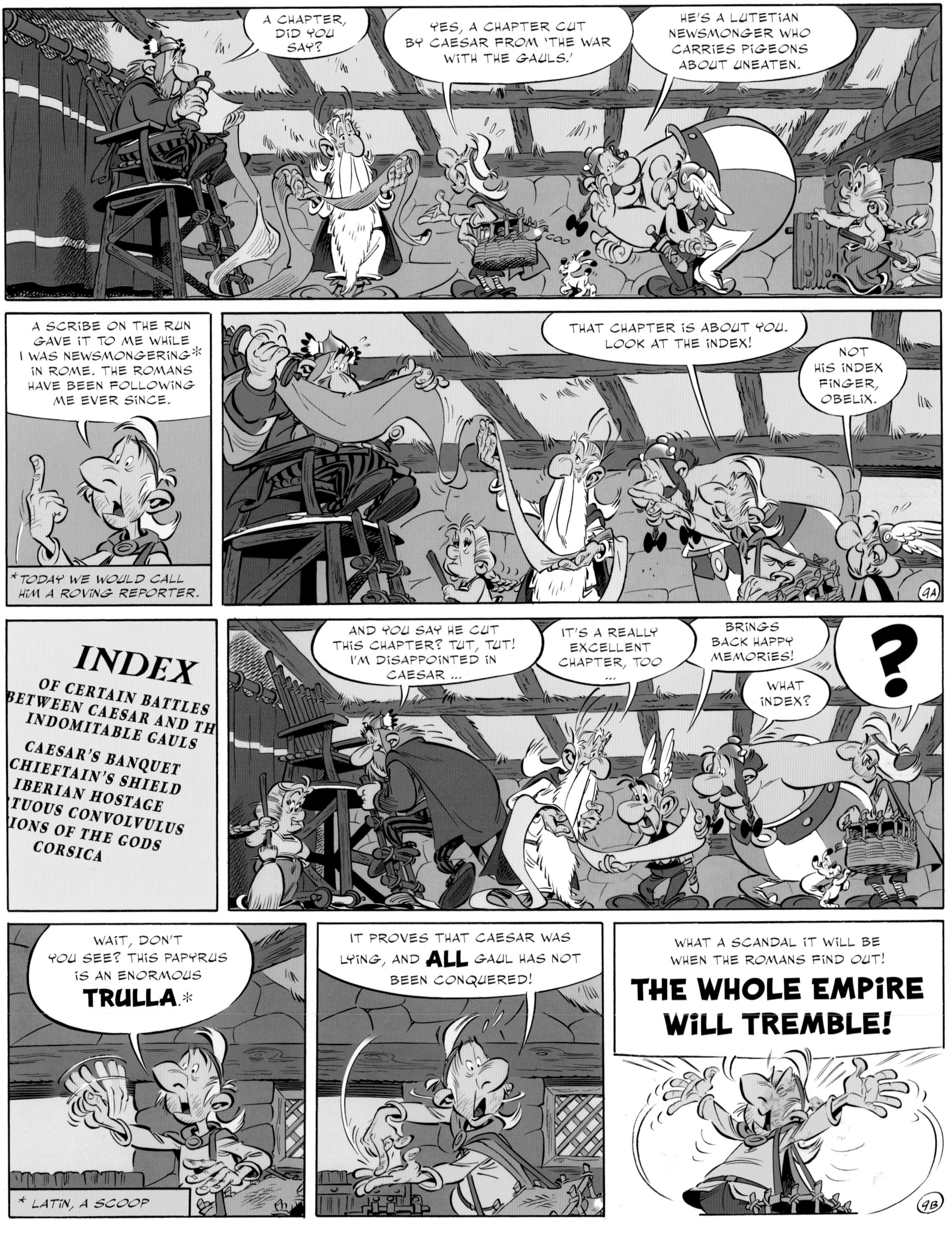

A CHAPTER, DID YOU SAY?
YES, A CHAPTER CUT BY CAESAR FROM 'THE WAR WITH THE GAULS.'
HE'S A LUTETIAN NEWSMONGER WHO CARRIES PIGEONS ABOUT UNEATEN.
A SCRIBE ON THE RUN GAVE IT TO ME WHILE I WAS NEWSMONGERING* IN ROME. THE ROMANS HAVE BEEN FOLLOWING ME EVER SINCE.
* TODAY WE WOULD CALL HIM A ROVING REPORTER.
THAT CHAPTER IS ABOUT YOU. LOOK AT THE INDEX!
NOT HIS INDEX FINGER, OBELIX.
9A
INDEX
OF CERTAIN BATTLES
BETWEEN CAESAR AND TH
INDOMITABLE GAULS
CAESAR'S BANQUET
CHIEFTAIN'S SHIELD
IBERIAN HOSTAGE
TUOUS CONVOLVULUS
IONS OF THE GODS
CORSICA
AND YOU SAY HE CUT THIS CHAPTER? TUT, TUT! I'M DISAPPOINTED IN CAESAR ...
IT'S A REALLY EXCELLENT CHAPTER, TOO ...
BRINGS BACK HAPPY MEMORIES!
WHAT INDEX?
?
WAIT, DON'T YOU SEE? THIS PAPYRUS IS AN ENORMOUS TRULLA.*
* LATIN, A SCOOP
IT PROVES THAT CAESAR WAS LYING, AND ALL GAUL HAS NOT BEEN CONQUERED!
WHAT A SCANDAL IT WILL BE WHEN THE ROMANS FIND OUT!
THE WHOLE EMPIRE WILL TREMBLE!
9B

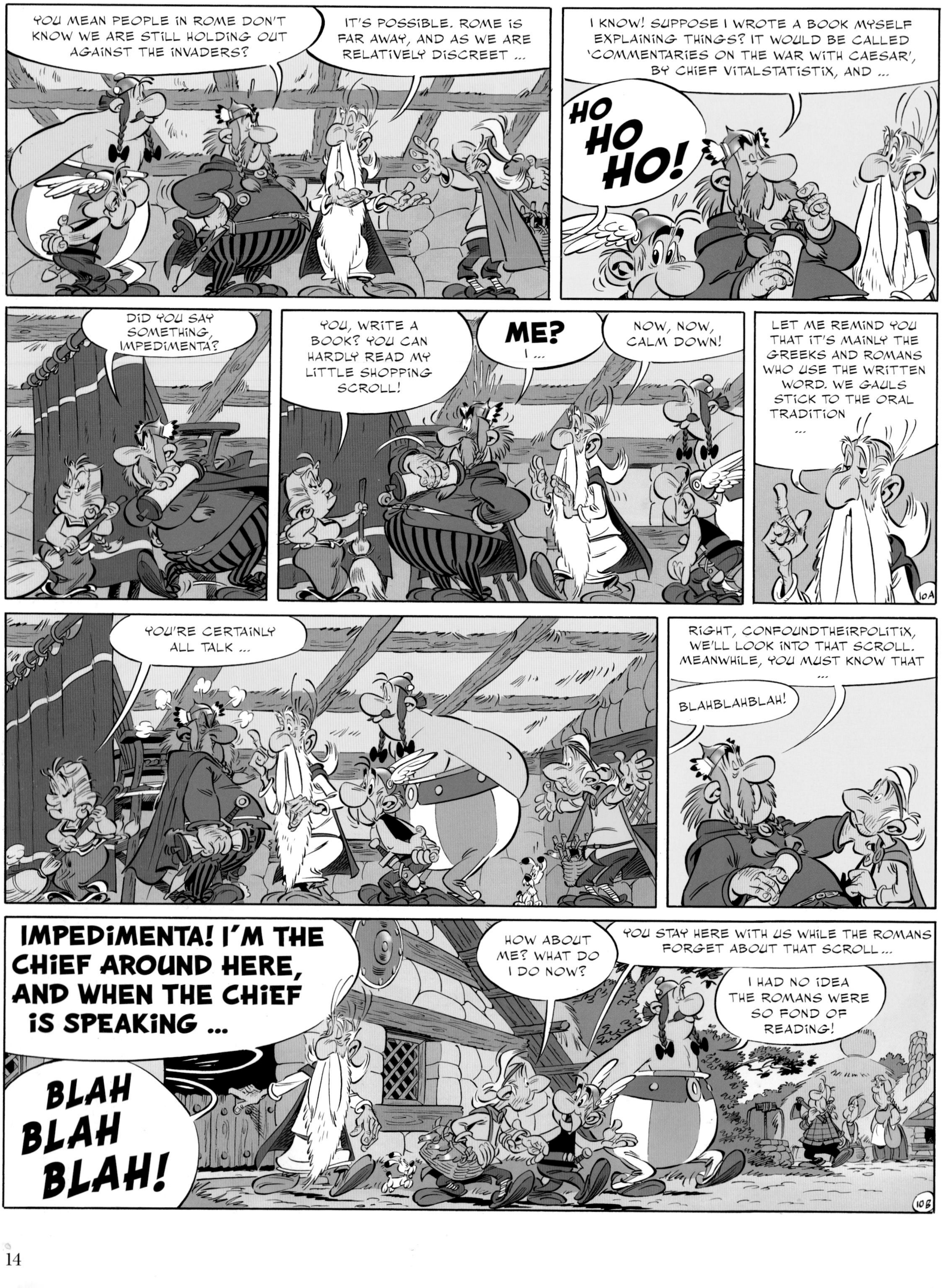
YOU MEAN PEOPLE IN ROME DON'T KNOW WE ARE STILL HOLDING OUT AGAINST THE INVADERS?
IT'S POSSIBLE. ROME IS FAR AWAY, AND AS WE ARE RELATIVELY DISCREET ...
I KNOW! SUPPOSE I WROTE A BOOK MYSELF EXPLAINING THINGS? IT WOULD BE CALLED 'COMMENTARIES ON THE WAR WITH CAESAR', BY CHIEF VITALSTATISTIX, AND ...
HO HO HO!
DID YOU SAY SOMETHING, IMPEDIMENTA?
YOU, WRITE A BOOK? YOU CAN HARDLY READ MY LITTLE SHOPPING SCROLL!
ME? I ...
NOW, NOW, CALM DOWN!
LET ME REMIND YOU THAT IT'S MAINLY THE GREEKS AND ROMANS WHO USE THE WRITTEN WORD. WE GAULS STICK TO THE ORAL TRADITION ...
10A
YOU'RE CERTAINLY ALL TALK ...
RIGHT, CONFOUNDTHEIRPOLITIX, WE'LL LOOK INTO THAT SCROLL. MEANWHILE, YOU MUST KNOW THAT ...
BLAHBLAHBLAH!
IMPEDIMENTA! I'M THE CHIEF AROUND HERE, AND WHEN THE CHIEF IS SPEAKING ...
BLAH BLAH BLAH!
HOW ABOUT ME? WHAT DO I DO NOW?
YOU STAY HERE WITH US WHILE THE ROMANS FORGET ABOUT THAT SCROLL ...
I HAD NO IDEA THE ROMANS WERE SO FOND OF READING!
10B

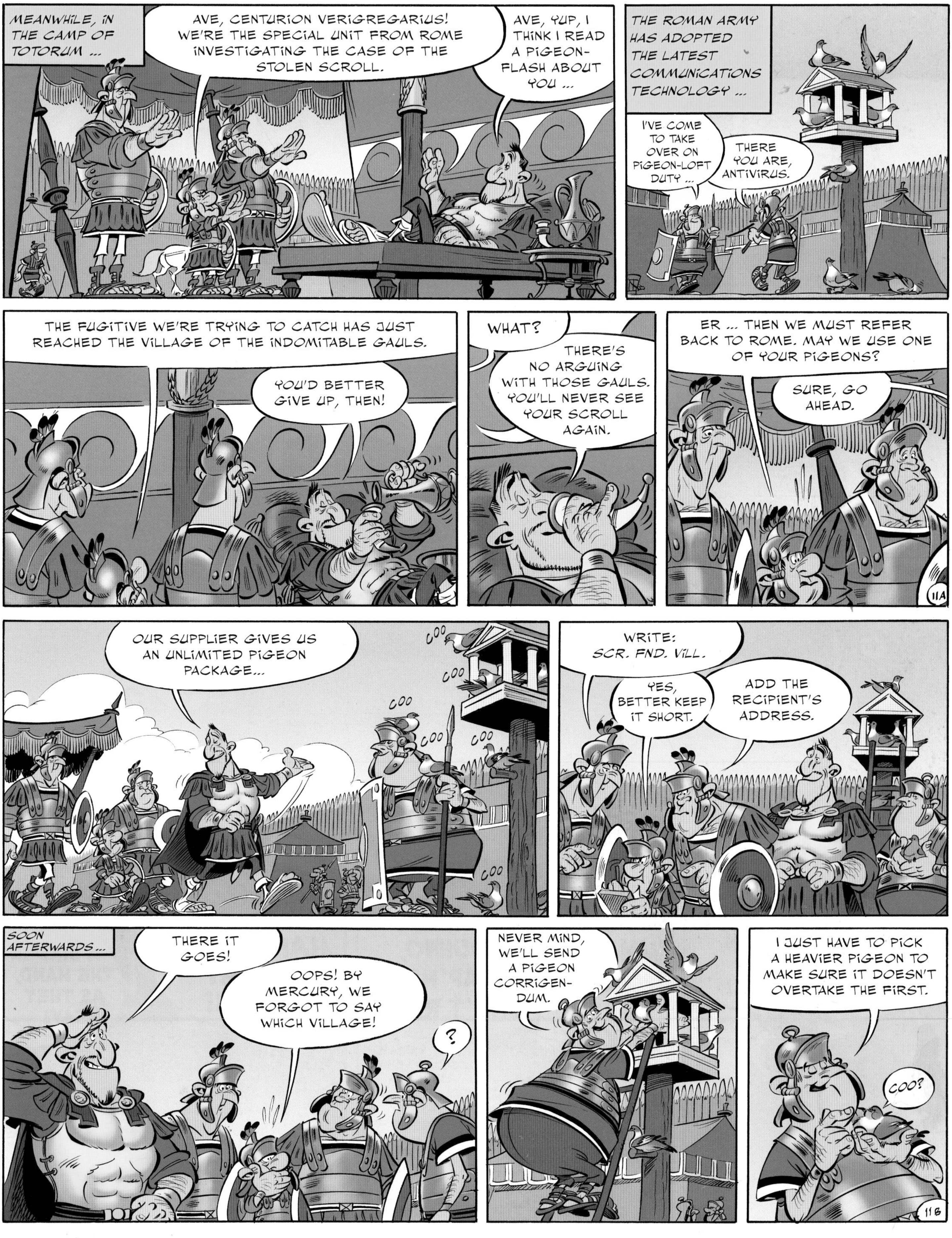
MEANWHILE, IN THE CAMP OF TOTORUM ...
AVE, CENTURION VERIGREGARIUS! WE'RE THE SPECIAL UNIT FROM ROME INVESTIGATING THE CASE OF THE STOLEN SCROLL.
AVE, YUP, I THINK I READ A PIGEON-FLASH ABOUT YOU ...
THE ROMAN ARMY HAS ADOPTED THE LATEST COMMUNICATIONS TECHNOLOGY ...
I'VE COME TO TAKE OVER ON PIGEON-LOFT DUTY ...
THERE YOU ARE, ANTIVIRUS.
THE FUGITIVE WE'RE TRYING TO CATCH HAS JUST REACHED THE VILLAGE OF THE INDOMITABLE GAULS.
YOU'D BETTER GIVE UP, THEN!
WHAT?
THERE'S NO ARGUING WITH THOSE GAULS. YOU'LL NEVER SEE YOUR SCROLL AGAIN.
ER ... THEN WE MUST REFER BACK TO ROME. MAY WE USE ONE OF YOUR PIGEONS?
SURE, GO AHEAD.
11A
OUR SUPPLIER GIVES US AN UNLIMITED PIGEON PACKAGE...
COO
COO
COO
COO
COO
COO
WRITE: SCR. FND. VILL.
YES, BETTER KEEP IT SHORT.
ADD THE RECIPIENT'S ADDRESS.
SOON AFTERWARDS...
THERE IT GOES!
OOPS! BY MERCURY, WE FORGOT TO SAY WHICH VILLAGE!
?
NEVER MIND, WE'LL SEND A PIGEON CORRIGEN-DUM.
I JUST HAVE TO PICK A HEAVIER PIGEON TO MAKE SURE IT DOESN'T OVERTAKE THE FIRST.
COO?
11B

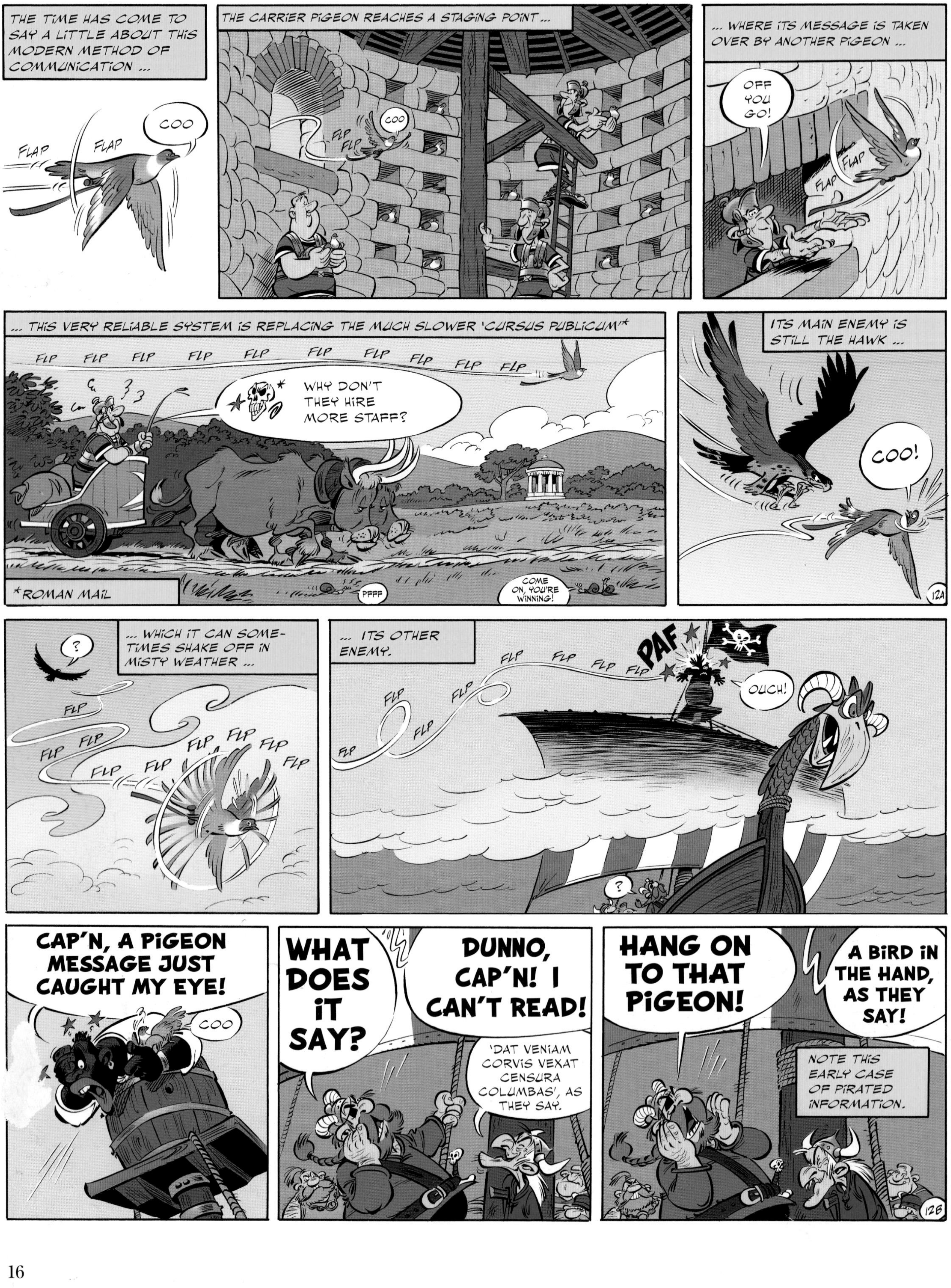
THE TIME HAS COME TO SAY A LITTLE ABOUT THIS MODERN METHOD OF COMMUNICATION ...
FLAP
FLAP
COO
THE CARRIER PIGEON REACHES A STAGING POINT ...
FLP
FLP
COO
... WHERE ITS MESSAGE IS TAKEN OVER BY ANOTHER PIGEON ...
OFF YOU GO!
FLAP
FLAP
... THIS VERY RELIABLE SYSTEM IS REPLACING THE MUCH SLOWER 'CURSUS PUBLICUM'*
FLP FLP FLP FLP FLP FLP FLP FLP FLP FLP
WHY DON'T THEY HIRE MORE STAFF?
*ROMAN MAIL
PFFF
COME ON, YOU'RE WINNING!
ITS MAIN ENEMY IS STILL THE HAWK ...
COO!
... WHICH IT CAN SOMETIMES SHAKE OFF IN MISTY WEATHER ...
?
FLP
FLP FLP
FLP FLP FLP FLP
FLP FLP
... ITS OTHER ENEMY.
FLP FLP FLP FLP
FLP FLP FLP FLP
PAF
OUCH!
?
CAP'N, A PIGEON MESSAGE JUST CAUGHT MY EYE!
COO
WHAT DOES IT SAY?
DUNNO, CAP'N! I CAN'T READ!
'DAT VENIAM CORVIS VEXAT CENSURA COLUMBAS', AS THEY SAY.
HANG ON TO THAT PIGEON!
A BIRD IN THE HAND, AS THEY SAY!
NOTE THIS EARLY CASE OF PIRATED INFORMATION.

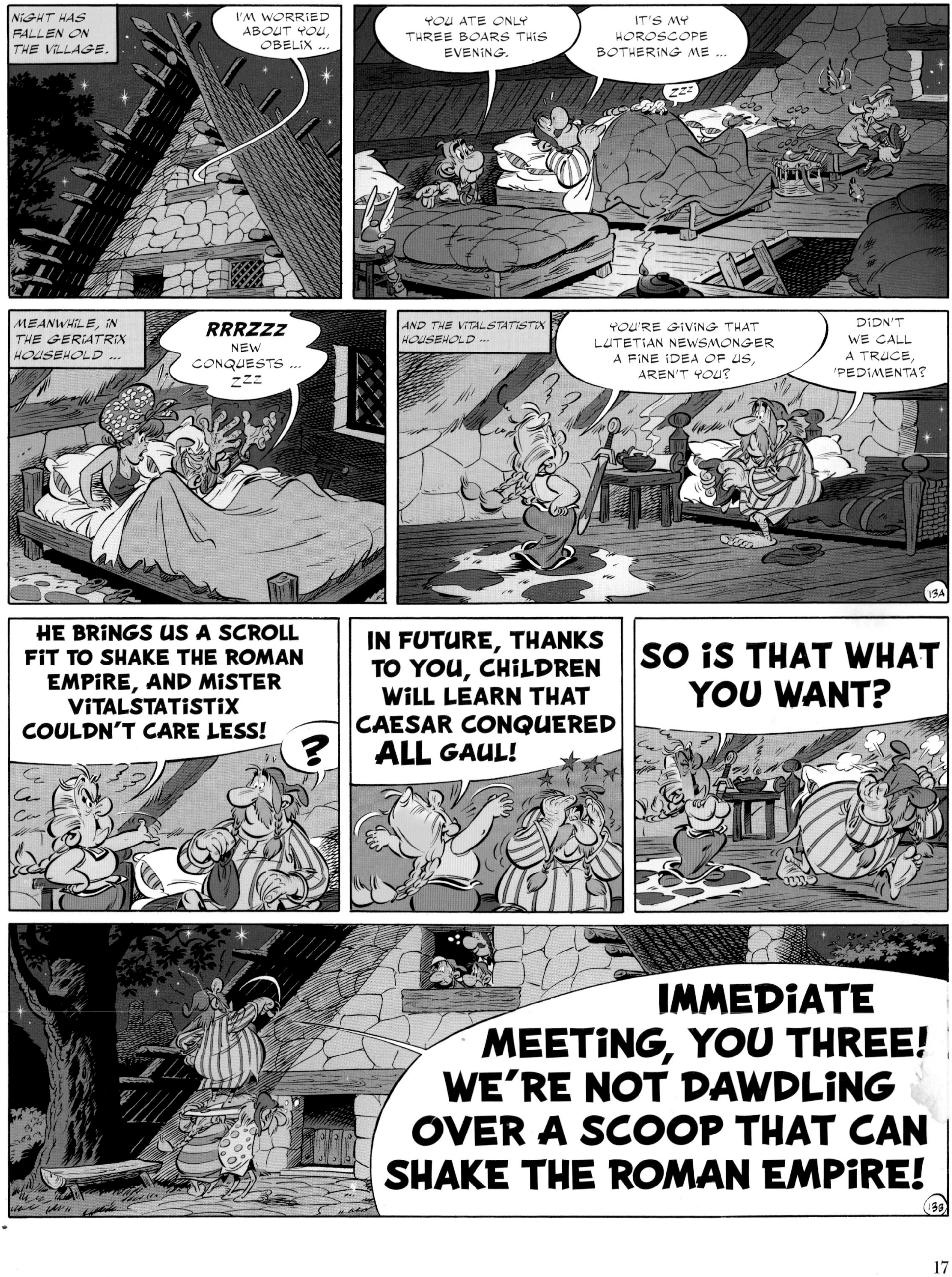
NIGHT HAS FALLEN ON THE VILLAGE.
I'M WORRIED ABOUT YOU, OBELIX ...
YOU ATE ONLY THREE BOARS THIS EVENING.
IT'S MY HOROSCOPE BOTHERING ME ...
ZZZ
MEANWHILE, IN THE GERIATRIX HOUSEHOLD ...
RRRZZZ NEW CONQUESTS ... ZZZ
AND THE VITALSTATISTIX HOUSEHOLD ...
YOU'RE GIVING THAT LUTETIAN NEWSMONGER A FINE IDEA OF US, AREN'T YOU?
DIDN'T WE CALL A TRUCE, 'PEDIMENTA?
13A
HE BRINGS US A SCROLL FIT TO SHAKE THE ROMAN EMPIRE, AND MISTER VITALSTATISTIX COULDN'T CARE LESS!
?
IN FUTURE, THANKS TO YOU, CHILDREN WILL LEARN THAT CAESAR CONQUERED ALL GAUL!
SO IS THAT WHAT YOU WANT?
IMMEDIATE MEETING, YOU THREE! WE'RE NOT DAWDLING OVER A SCOOP THAT CAN SHAKE THE ROMAN EMPIRE!
13B

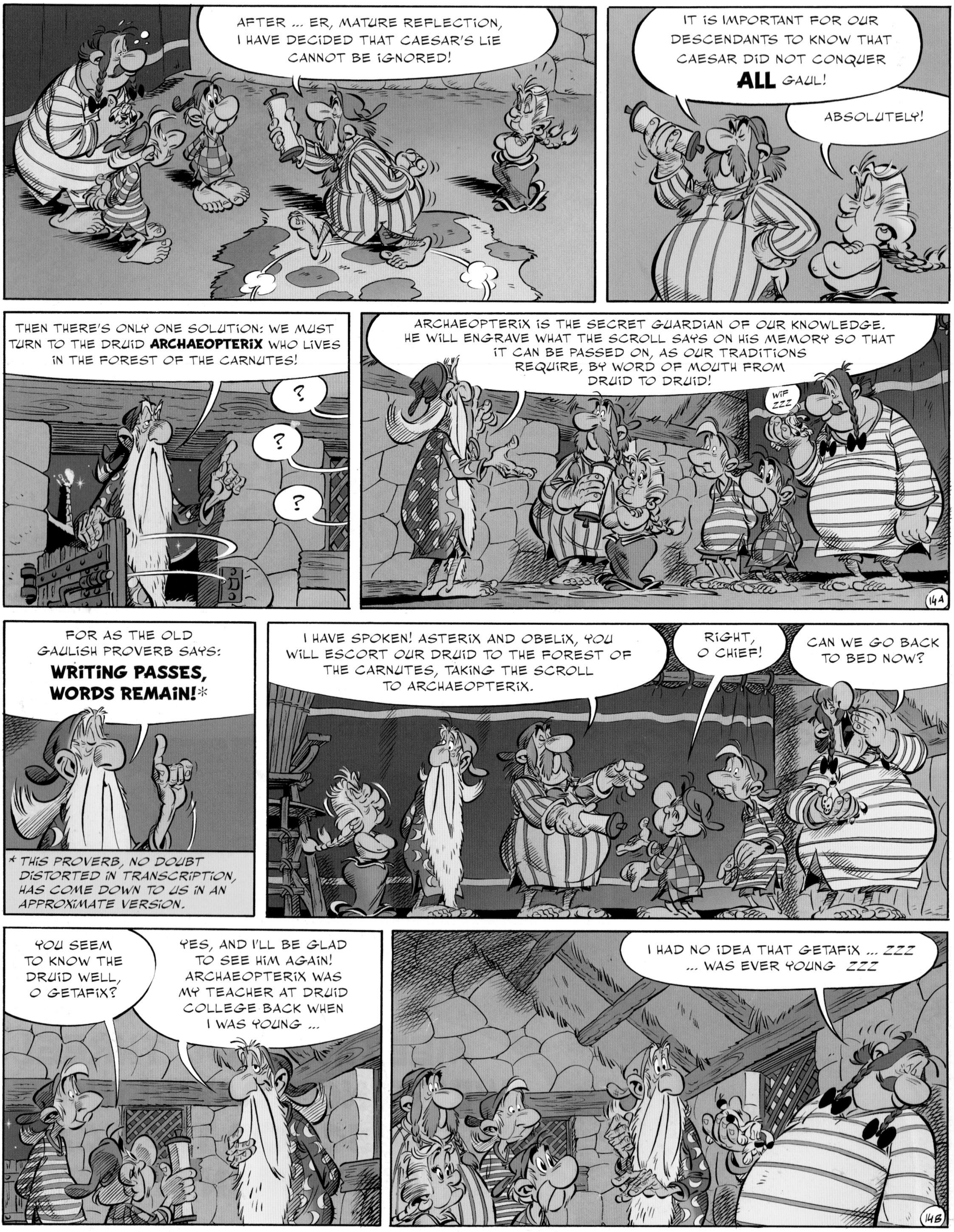
AFTER ... ER, MATURE REFLECTION, I HAVE DECIDED THAT CAESAR'S LIE CANNOT BE IGNORED!
IT IS IMPORTANT FOR OUR DESCENDANTS TO KNOW THAT CAESAR DID NOT CONQUER ALL GAUL!
ABSOLUTELY!
THEN THERE'S ONLY ONE SOLUTION: WE MUST TURN TO THE DRUID ARCHAEOPTERIX WHO LIVES IN THE FOREST OF THE CARNUTES!
?
?
?
ARCHAEOPTERIX IS THE SECRET GUARDIAN OF OUR KNOWLEDGE. HE WILL ENGRAVE WHAT THE SCROLL SAYS ON HIS MEMORY SO THAT IT CAN BE PASSED ON, AS OUR TRADITIONS REQUIRE, BY WORD OF MOUTH FROM DRUID TO DRUID!
WIF ZZZ
14A
FOR AS THE OLD GAULISH PROVERB SAYS: WRITING PASSES, WORDS REMAIN!*
* THIS PROVERB, NO DOUBT DISTORTED IN TRANSCRIPTION, HAS COME DOWN TO US IN AN APPROXIMATE VERSION.
I HAVE SPOKEN! ASTERIX AND OBELIX, YOU WILL ESCORT OUR DRUID TO THE FOREST OF THE CARNUTES, TAKING THE SCROLL TO ARCHAEOPTERIX.
RIGHT, O CHIEF!
CAN WE GO BACK TO BED NOW?
YOU SEEM TO KNOW THE DRUID WELL, O GETAFIX?
YES, AND I'LL BE GLAD TO SEE HIM AGAIN! ARCHAEOPTERIX WAS MY TEACHER AT DRUID COLLEGE BACK WHEN I WAS YOUNG ...
I HAD NO IDEA THAT GETAFIX ... ZZZ ... WAS EVER YOUNG ZZZ
14B

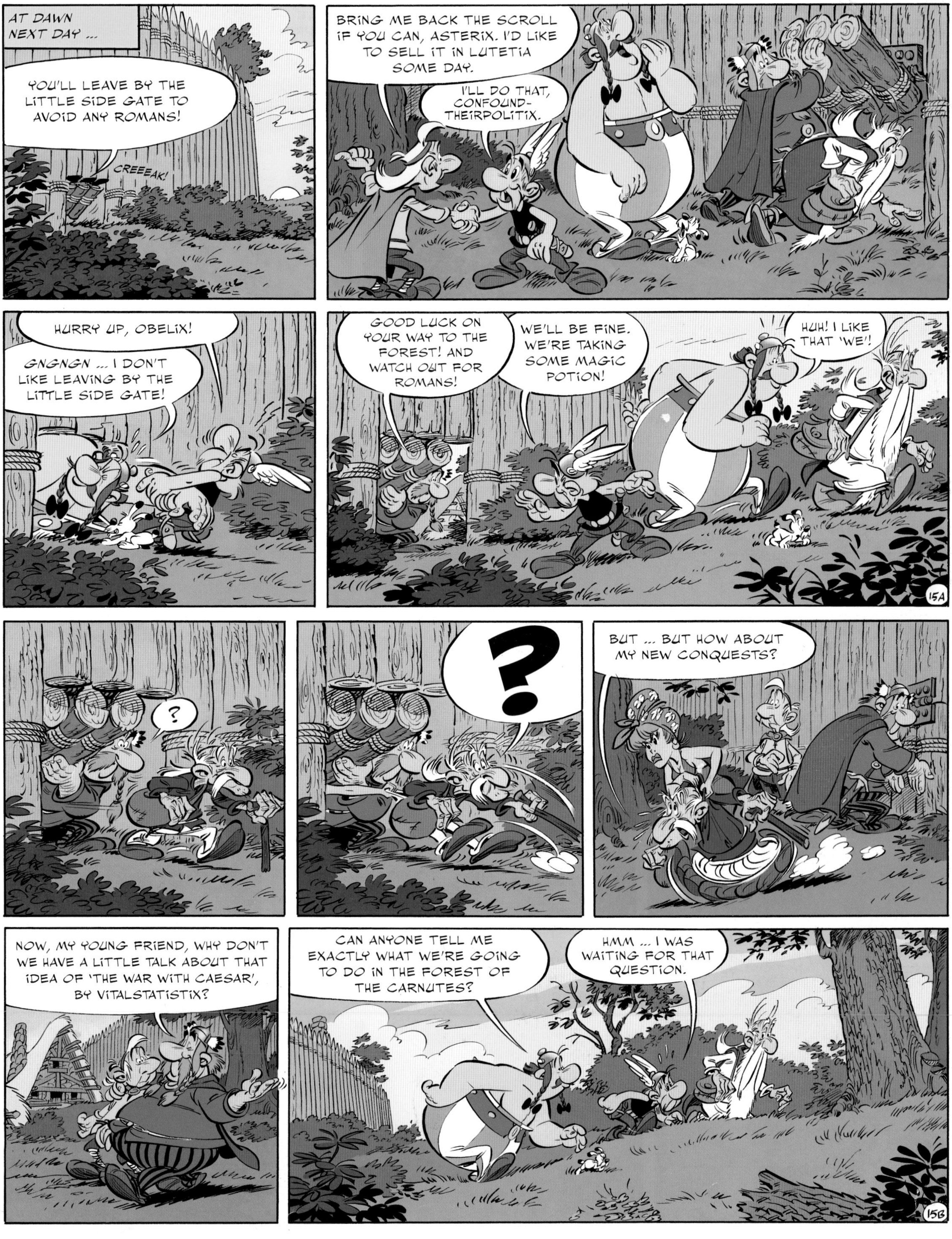
AT DAWN NEXT DAY ...
YOU'LL LEAVE BY THE LITTLE SIDE GATE TO AVOID ANY ROMANS!
CREEEAK!
BRING ME BACK THE SCROLL IF YOU CAN, ASTERIX. I'D LIKE TO SELL IT IN LUTETIA SOME DAY.
I'LL DO THAT, CONFOUND-THEIRPOLITIX.
HURRY UP, OBELIX!
GNGNGN ... I DON'T LIKE LEAVING BY THE LITTLE SIDE GATE!
GOOD LUCK ON YOUR WAY TO THE FOREST! AND WATCH OUT FOR ROMANS!
WE'LL BE FINE. WE'RE TAKING SOME MAGIC POTION!
HUH! I LIKE THAT 'WE'!
15A
?
?
BUT ... BUT HOW ABOUT MY NEW CONQUESTS?
NOW, MY YOUNG FRIEND, WHY DON'T WE HAVE A LITTLE TALK ABOUT THAT IDEA OF 'THE WAR WITH CAESAR', BY VITALSTATISTIX?
CAN ANYONE TELL ME EXACTLY WHAT WE'RE GOING TO DO IN THE FOREST OF THE CARNUTES?
HMM ... I WAS WAITING FOR THAT QUESTION.
15B

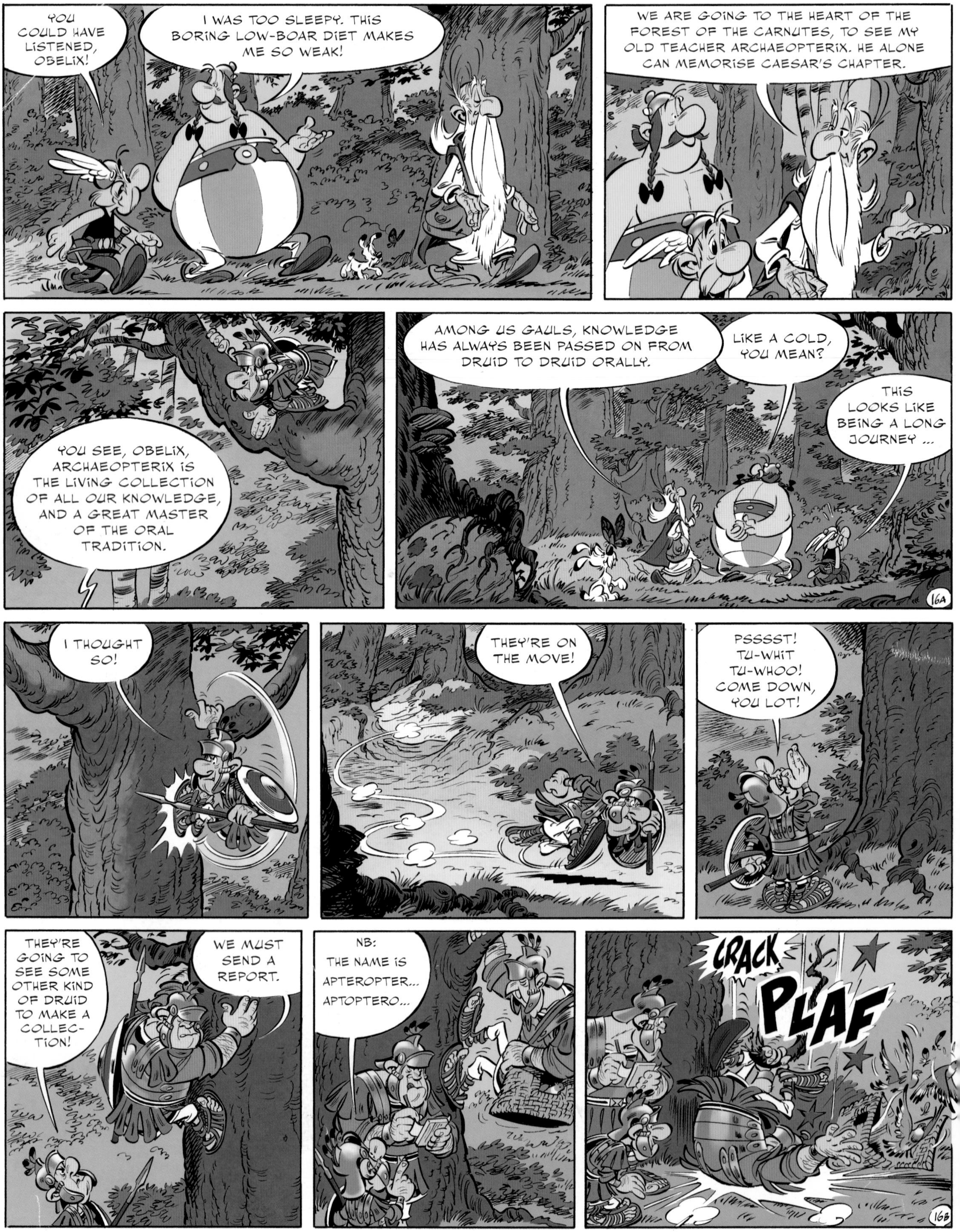
YOU COULD HAVE LISTENED, OBELIX!
I WAS TOO SLEEPY. THIS BORING LOW-BOAR DIET MAKES ME SO WEAK!
WE ARE GOING TO THE HEART OF THE FOREST OF THE CARNUTES, TO SEE MY OLD TEACHER ARCHAEOPTERIX. HE ALONE CAN MEMORISE CAESAR'S CHAPTER.
YOU SEE, OBELIX, ARCHAEOPTERIX IS THE LIVING COLLECTION OF ALL OUR KNOWLEDGE, AND A GREAT MASTER OF THE ORAL TRADITION.
AMONG US GAULS, KNOWLEDGE HAS ALWAYS BEEN PASSED ON FROM DRUID TO DRUID ORALLY.
LIKE A COLD, YOU MEAN?
THIS LOOKS LIKE BEING A LONG JOURNEY ...
16A
I THOUGHT SO!
THEY'RE ON THE MOVE!
PSSSST! TU-WHIT TU-WHOO! COME DOWN, YOU LOT!
THEY'RE GOING TO SEE SOME OTHER KIND OF DRUID TO MAKE A COLLEC-TION!
WE MUST SEND A REPORT.
NB: THE NAME IS APTEROPTER... APTOPTERO...
CRACK
PLAF
16B

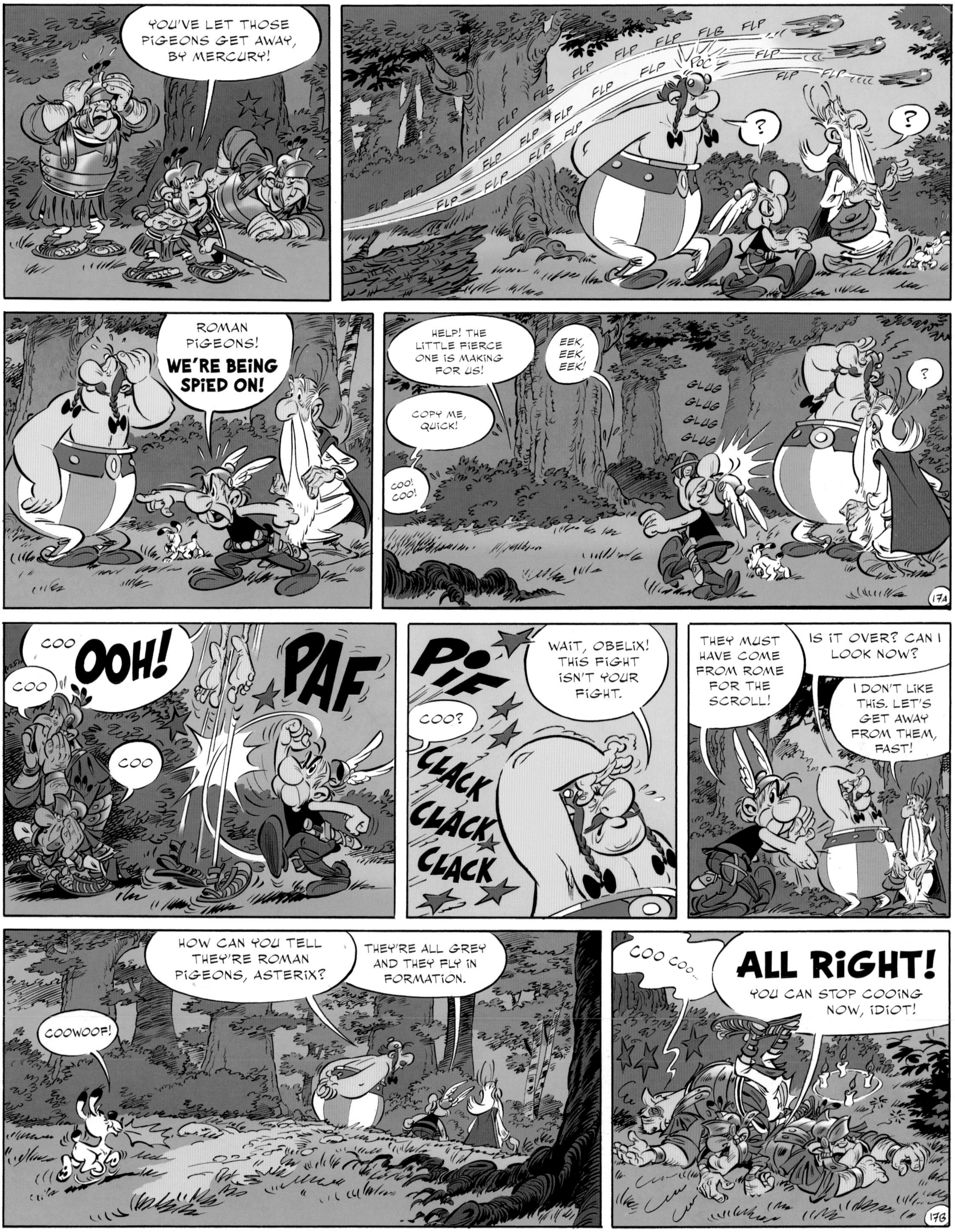
YOU'VE LET THOSE PIGEONS GET AWAY, BY MERCURY!
FLP FLP FLP FLB FLP
POC
?
?
ROMAN PIGEONS! WE'RE BEING SPIED ON!
HELP! THE LITTLE FIERCE ONE IS MAKING FOR US!
EEK, EEK, EEK!
COPY ME, QUICK!
COO! COO!
GLUG GLUG GLUG GLUG
?
COO
COO
OOH!
PAF
COO
PIF
COO?
CLACK CLACK CLACK
WAIT, OBELIX! THIS FIGHT ISN'T YOUR FIGHT.
THEY MUST HAVE COME FROM ROME FOR THE SCROLL!
IS IT OVER? CAN I LOOK NOW?
I DON'T LIKE THIS. LET'S GET AWAY FROM THEM, FAST!
HOW CAN YOU TELL THEY'RE ROMAN PIGEONS, ASTERIX?
THEY'RE ALL GREY AND THEY FLY IN FORMATION.
COOWOOF!
COO COO...
ALL RIGHT! YOU CAN STOP COOING NOW, IDIOT!

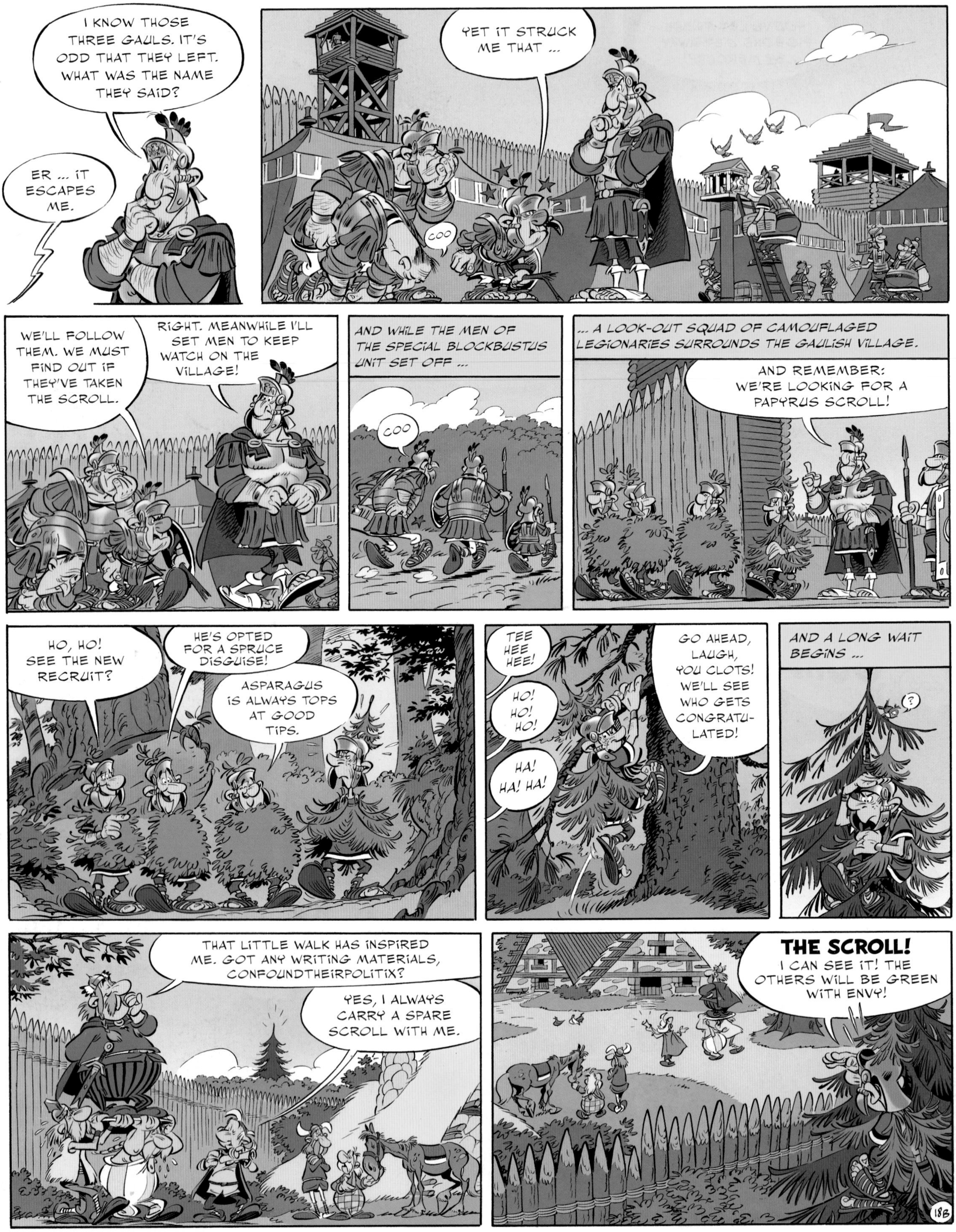
I KNOW THOSE THREE GAULS. IT'S ODD THAT THEY LEFT. WHAT WAS THE NAME THEY SAID?
ER ... IT ESCAPES ME.
YET IT STRUCK ME THAT ...
COO
WE'LL FOLLOW THEM. WE MUST FIND OUT IF THEY'VE TAKEN THE SCROLL.
RIGHT. MEANWHILE I'LL SET MEN TO KEEP WATCH ON THE VILLAGE!
AND WHILE THE MEN OF THE SPECIAL BLOCKBUSTUS UNIT SET OFF ...
COO
... A LOOK-OUT SQUAD OF CAMOUFLAGED LEGIONARIES SURROUNDS THE GAULISH VILLAGE.
AND REMEMBER: WE'RE LOOKING FOR A PAPYRUS SCROLL!
HO, HO! SEE THE NEW RECRUIT?
HE'S OPTED FOR A SPRUCE DISGUISE!
ASPARAGUS IS ALWAYS TOPS AT GOOD TIPS.
TEE HEE HEE!
HO! HO! HO!
HA! HA! HA!
GO AHEAD, LAUGH, YOU CLOTS! WE'LL SEE WHO GETS CONGRATU-LATED!
AND A LONG WAIT BEGINS ...
?
THAT LITTLE WALK HAS INSPIRED ME. GOT ANY WRITING MATERIALS, CONFOUNDTHEIRPOLITIX?
YES, I ALWAYS CARRY A SPARE SCROLL WITH ME.
THE SCROLL! I CAN SEE IT! THE OTHERS WILL BE GREEN WITH ENVY!

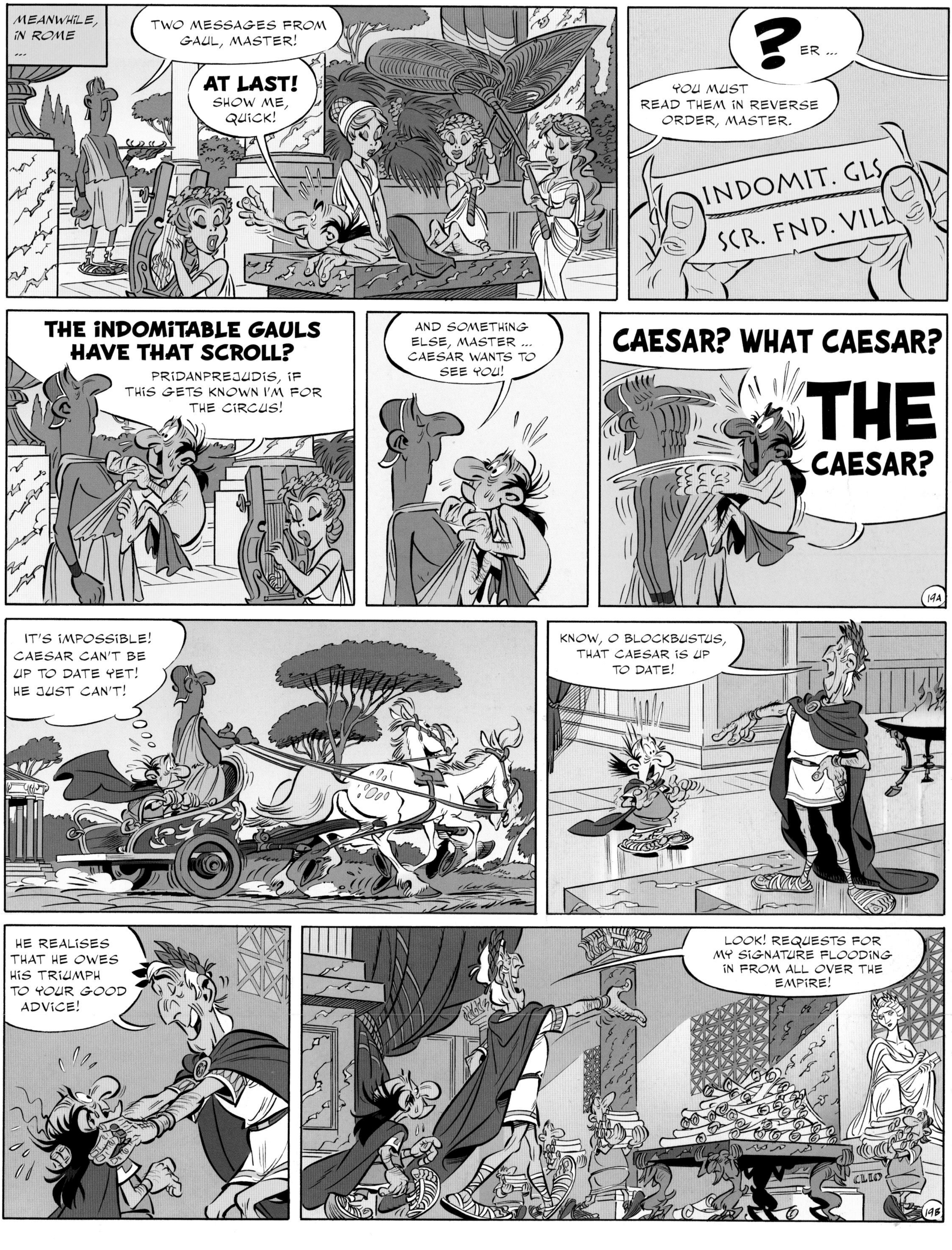
MEANWHILE, IN ROME ...
TWO MESSAGES FROM GAUL, MASTER!
AT LAST! SHOW ME, QUICK!
? ER ...
YOU MUST READ THEM IN REVERSE ORDER, MASTER.
INDOMIT. GLS
SCR. FND. VILL
THE INDOMITABLE GAULS HAVE THAT SCROLL?
PRIDANPREJUDIS, IF THIS GETS KNOWN I'M FOR THE CIRCUS!
AND SOMETHING ELSE, MASTER ... CAESAR WANTS TO SEE YOU!
CAESAR? WHAT CAESAR? THE CAESAR?
19A
IT'S IMPOSSIBLE! CAESAR CAN'T BE UP TO DATE YET! HE JUST CAN'T!
KNOW, O BLOCKBUSTUS, THAT CAESAR IS UP TO DATE!
HE REALISES THAT HE OWES HIS TRIUMPH TO YOUR GOOD ADVICE!
LOOK! REQUESTS FOR MY SIGNATURE FLOODING IN FROM ALL OVER THE EMPIRE!
CLIO
19B

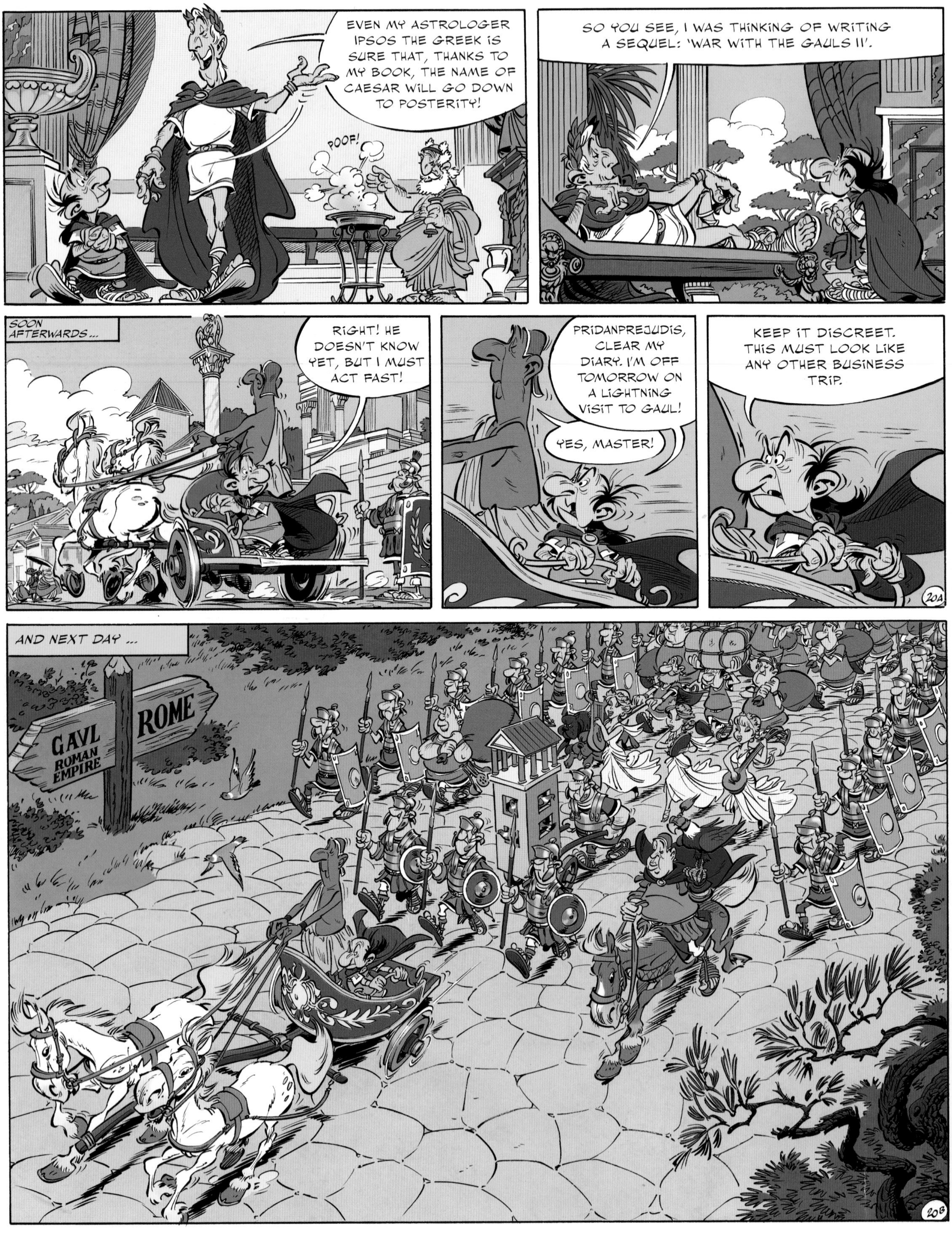

EVEN MY ASTROLOGER IPSOS THE GREEK IS SURE THAT, THANKS TO MY BOOK, THE NAME OF CAESAR WILL GO DOWN TO POSTERITY!
POOF!
SO YOU SEE, I WAS THINKING OF WRITING A SEQUEL: 'WAR WITH THE GAULS II'.
SOON AFTERWARDS...
RIGHT! HE DOESN'T KNOW YET, BUT I MUST ACT FAST!
PRIDANPREJUDIS, CLEAR MY DIARY. I'M OFF TOMORROW ON A LIGHTNING VISIT TO GAUL!
YES, MASTER!
KEEP IT DISCREET. THIS MUST LOOK LIKE ANY OTHER BUSINESS TRIP.
20A
AND NEXT DAY ...
GAVL ROMAN EMPIRE
ROME
20B

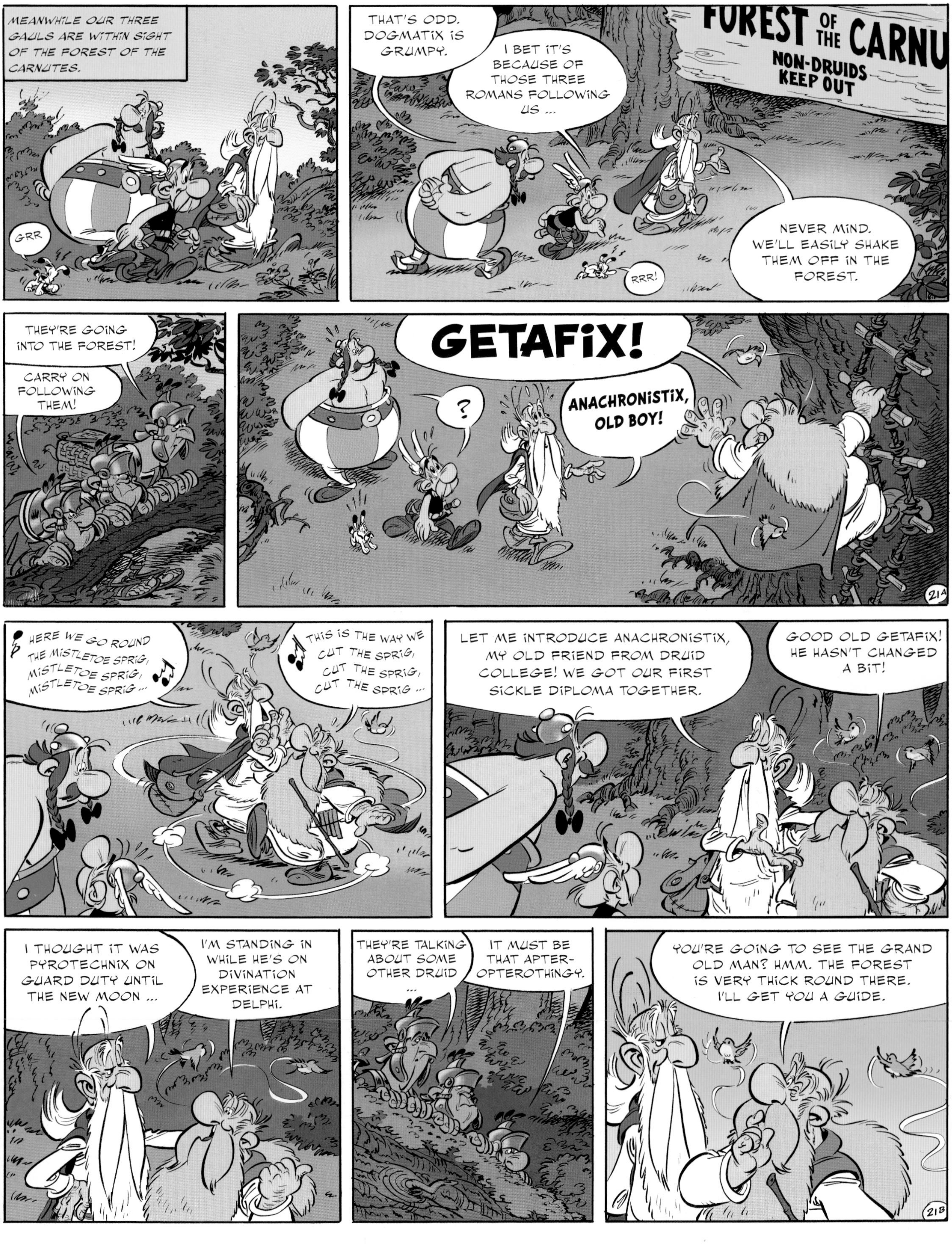
MEANWHILE OUR THREE GAULS ARE WITHIN SIGHT OF THE FOREST OF THE CARNUTES.
GRR
THAT'S ODD. DOGMATIX IS GRUMPY.
I BET IT'S BECAUSE OF THOSE THREE ROMANS FOLLOWING US ...
FOREST OF THE CARNU
NON-DRUIDS KEEP OUT
NEVER MIND. WE'LL EASILY SHAKE THEM OFF IN THE FOREST.
RRR!
THEY'RE GOING INTO THE FOREST!
CARRY ON FOLLOWING THEM!
GETAFIX!
?
ANACHRONISTIX, OLD BOY!
21A
HERE WE GO ROUND THE MISTLETOE SPRIG, MISTLETOE SPRIG, MISTLETOE SPRIG ...
THIS IS THE WAY WE CUT THE SPRIG, CUT THE SPRIG, CUT THE SPRIG ...
LET ME INTRODUCE ANACHRONISTIX, MY OLD FRIEND FROM DRUID COLLEGE! WE GOT OUR FIRST SICKLE DIPLOMA TOGETHER.
GOOD OLD GETAFIX! HE HASN'T CHANGED A BIT!
I THOUGHT IT WAS PYROTECHNIX ON GUARD DUTY UNTIL THE NEW MOON ...
I'M STANDING IN WHILE HE'S ON DIVINATION EXPERIENCE AT DELPHI.
THEY'RE TALKING ABOUT SOME OTHER DRUID ...
IT MUST BE THAT APTER-OPTEROTHINGY.
YOU'RE GOING TO SEE THE GRAND OLD MAN? HMM. THE FOREST IS VERY THICK ROUND THERE. I'LL GET YOU A GUIDE.
21B

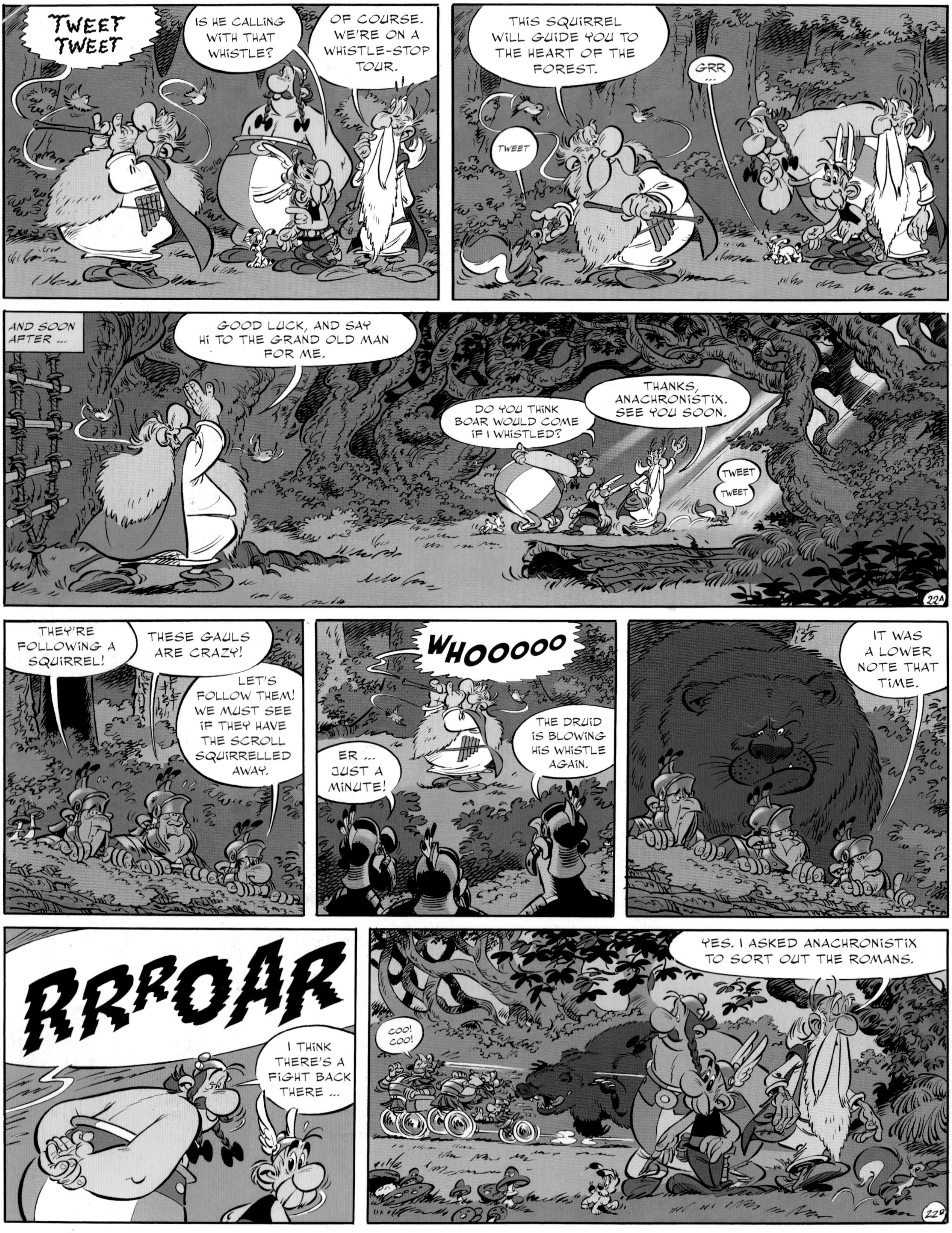

TWEET TWEET
IS HE CALLING WITH THAT WHISTLE?
OF COURSE. WE'RE ON A WHISTLE-STOP TOUR.
THIS SQUIRREL WILL GUIDE YOU TO THE HEART OF THE FOREST.
TWEET
GRR ...
AND SOON AFTER ...
GOOD LUCK, AND SAY HI TO THE GRAND OLD MAN FOR ME.
THANKS, ANACHRONISTIX. SEE YOU SOON.
DO YOU THINK BOAR WOULD COME IF I WHISTLED?
TWEET
TWEET
22A
THEY'RE FOLLOWING A SQUIRREL!
THESE GAULS ARE CRAZY!
LET'S FOLLOW THEM! WE MUST SEE IF THEY HAVE THE SCROLL SQUIRRELLED AWAY.
WHOOOOO
ER ... JUST A MINUTE!
THE DRUID IS BLOWING HIS WHISTLE AGAIN.
IT WAS A LOWER NOTE THAT TIME.
RRROAR
I THINK THERE'S A FIGHT BACK THERE ...
YES. I ASKED ANACHRONISTIX TO SORT OUT THE ROMANS.
COO! COO!
22B

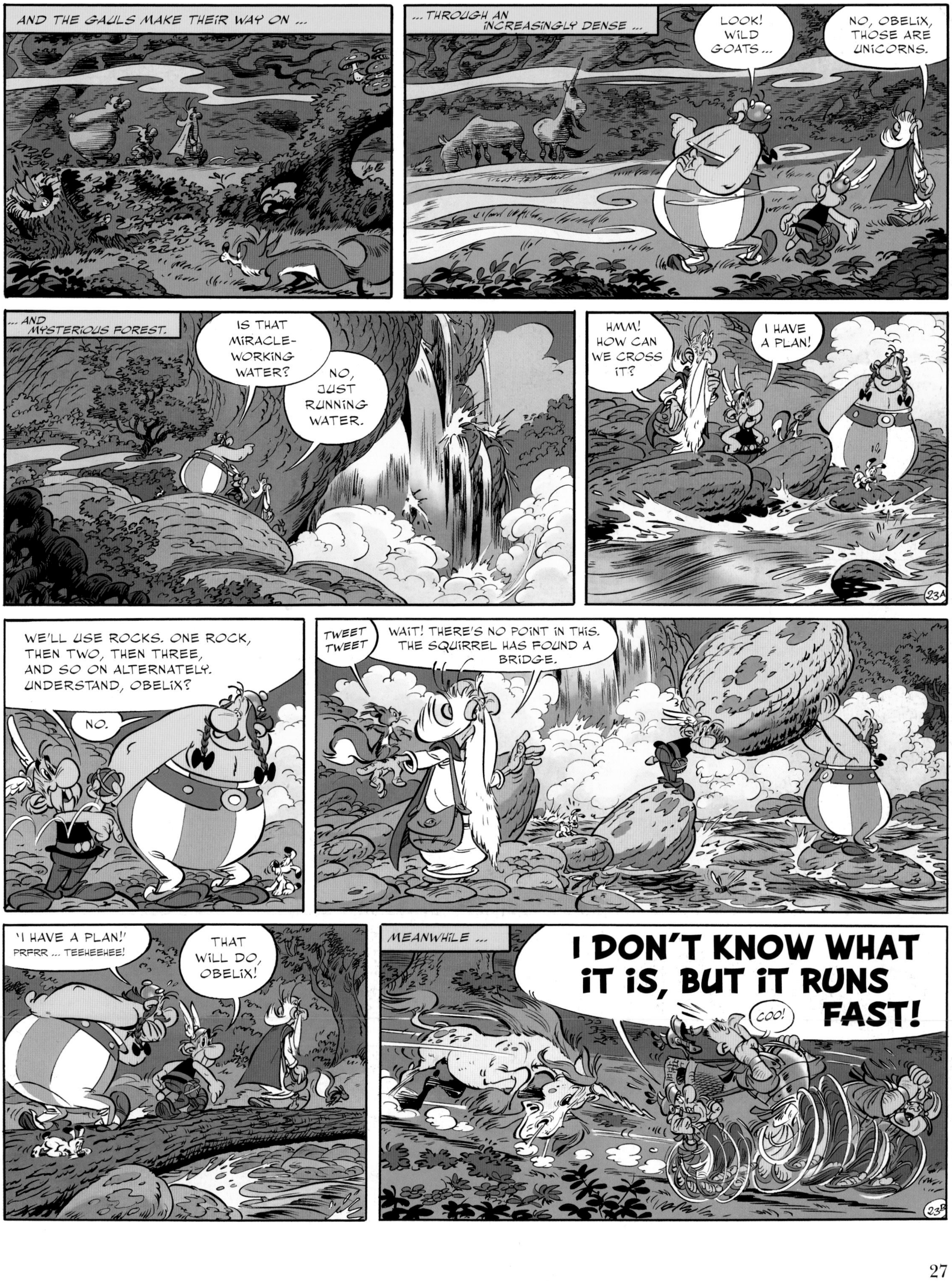
AND THE GAULS MAKE THEIR WAY ON ...
... THROUGH AN INCREASINGLY DENSE ...
LOOK! WILD GOATS ...
NO, OBELIX, THOSE ARE UNICORNS.
... AND MYSTERIOUS FOREST.
IS THAT MIRACLE-WORKING WATER?
NO, JUST RUNNING WATER.
HMM! HOW CAN WE CROSS IT?
I HAVE A PLAN!
23A
WE'LL USE ROCKS. ONE ROCK, THEN TWO, THEN THREE, AND SO ON ALTERNATELY. UNDERSTAND, OBELIX?
NO.
TWEET TWEET
WAIT! THERE'S NO POINT IN THIS. THE SQUIRREL HAS FOUND A BRIDGE.
'I HAVE A PLAN!' PRFRR ... TEEHEEHEE!
THAT WILL DO, OBELIX!
MEANWHILE ...
I DON'T KNOW WHAT IT IS, BUT IT RUNS FAST!
COO!
23B

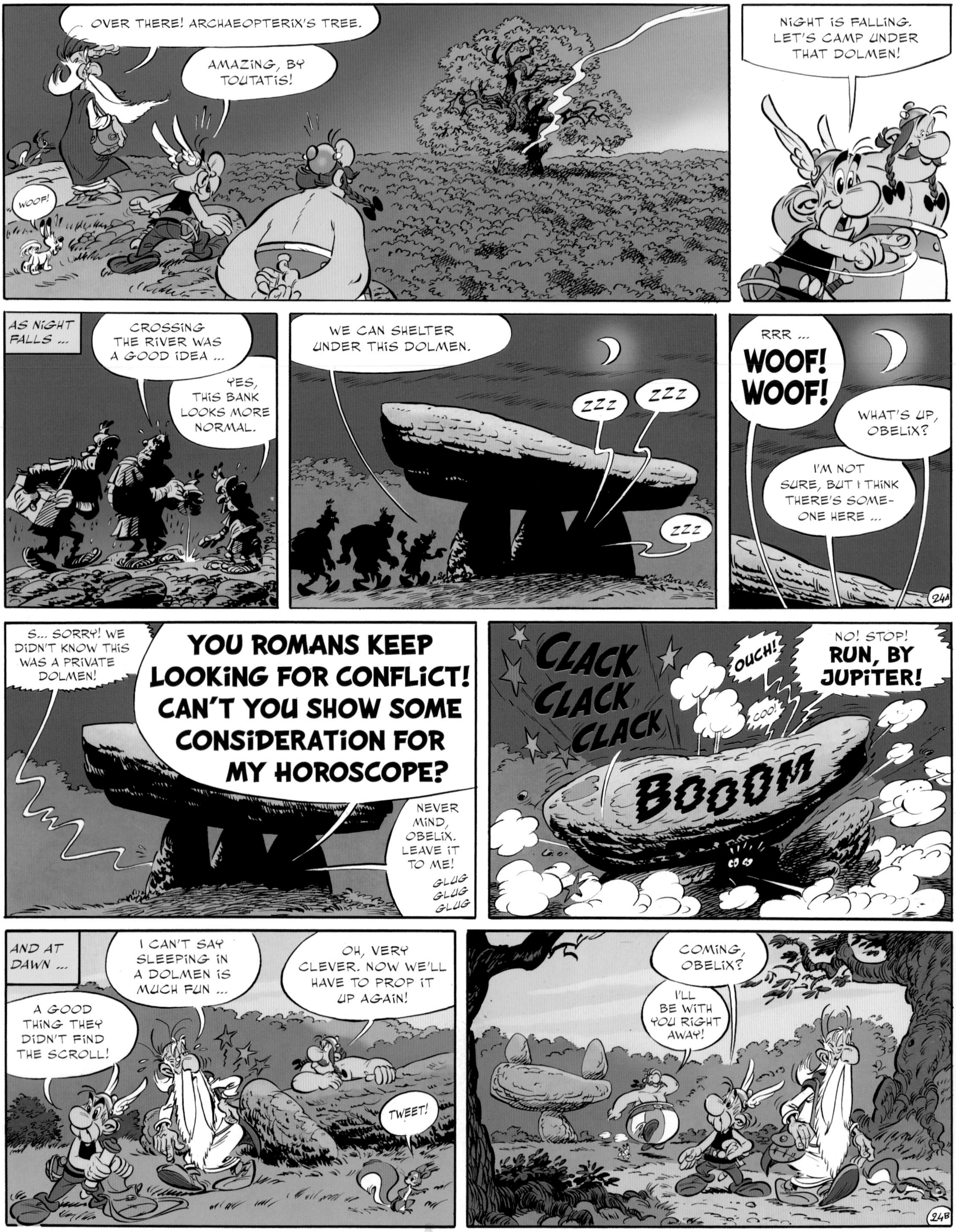
OVER THERE! ARCHAEOPTERIX'S TREE.
AMAZING, BY TOUTATIS!
WOOF!
NIGHT IS FALLING. LET'S CAMP UNDER THAT DOLMEN!
AS NIGHT FALLS ...
CROSSING THE RIVER WAS A GOOD IDEA ...
YES, THIS BANK LOOKS MORE NORMAL.
WE CAN SHELTER UNDER THIS DOLMEN.
ZZZ
ZZZ
ZZZ
RRR ...
WOOF! WOOF!
WHAT'S UP, OBELIX?
I'M NOT SURE, BUT I THINK THERE'S SOME-ONE HERE ...
24A
S... SORRY! WE DIDN'T KNOW THIS WAS A PRIVATE DOLMEN!
YOU ROMANS KEEP LOOKING FOR CONFLICT! CAN'T YOU SHOW SOME CONSIDERATION FOR MY HOROSCOPE?
NEVER MIND, OBELIX. LEAVE IT TO ME!
GLUG GLUG GLUG
CLACK CLACK CLACK
OUCH!
OOO!
NO! STOP! RUN, BY JUPITER!
BOOOM
AND AT DAWN ...
I CAN'T SAY SLEEPING IN A DOLMEN IS MUCH FUN ...
A GOOD THING THEY DIDN'T FIND THE SCROLL!
OH, VERY CLEVER. NOW WE'LL HAVE TO PROP IT UP AGAIN!
TWEET!
COMING, OBELIX?
I'LL BE WITH YOU RIGHT AWAY!
24B

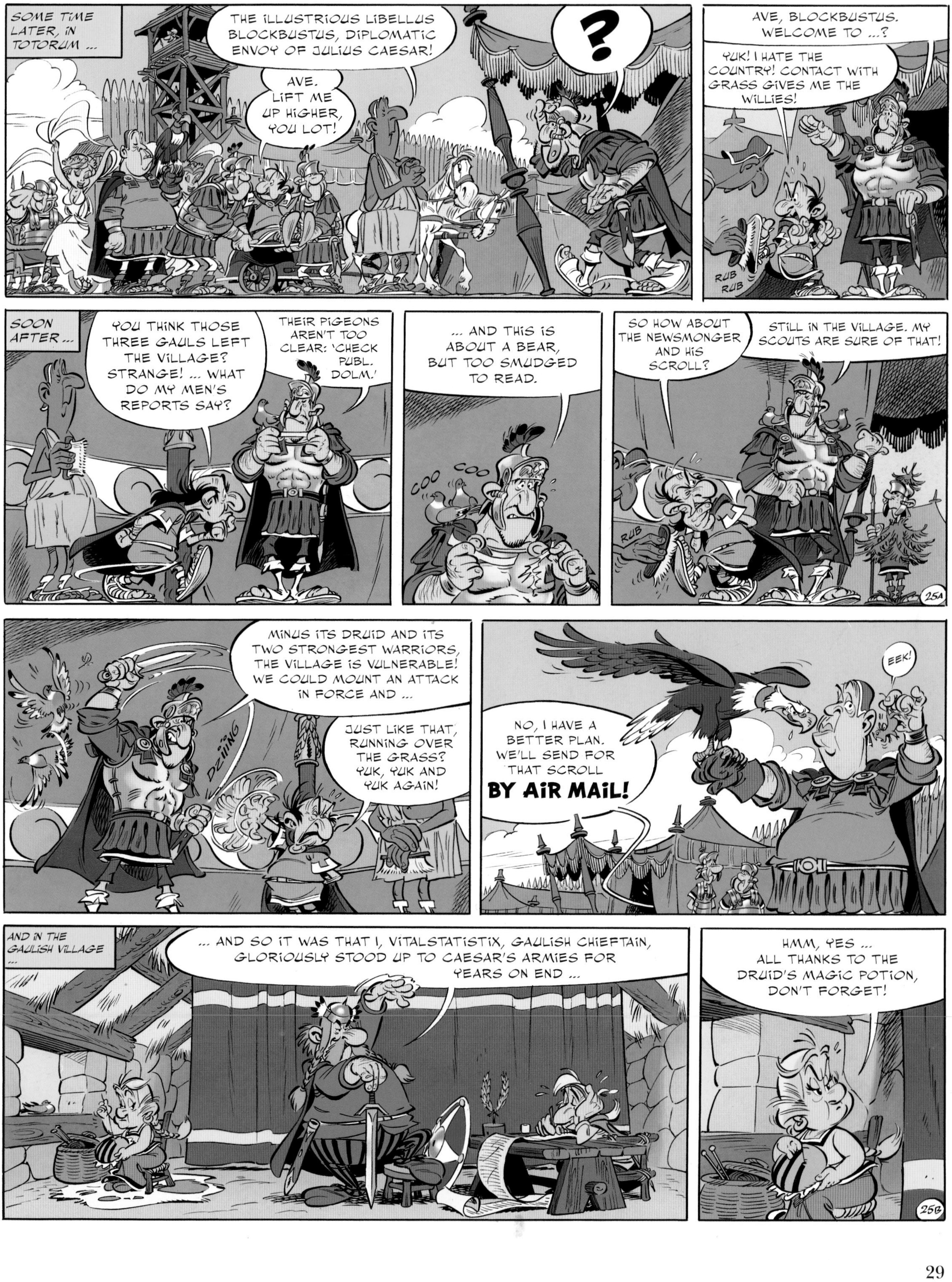

SOME TIME LATER, IN TOTORUM ...
THE ILLUSTRIOUS LIBELLUS BLOCKBUSTUS, DIPLOMATIC ENVOY OF JULIUS CAESAR!
AVE. LIFT ME UP HIGHER, YOU LOT!
?
AVE, BLOCKBUSTUS. WELCOME TO ...?
YUK! I HATE THE COUNTRY! CONTACT WITH GRASS GIVES ME THE WILLIES!
RUB RUB
SOON AFTER ...
YOU THINK THOSE THREE GAULS LEFT THE VILLAGE? STRANGE! ... WHAT DO MY MEN'S REPORTS SAY?
THEIR PIGEONS AREN'T TOO CLEAR: 'CHECK PUBL. DOLM.'
... AND THIS IS ABOUT A BEAR, BUT TOO SMUDGED TO READ.
COO COO
SO HOW ABOUT THE NEWSMONGER AND HIS SCROLL?
STILL IN THE VILLAGE. MY SCOUTS ARE SURE OF THAT!
RUB
25A
MINUS ITS DRUID AND ITS TWO STRONGEST WARRIORS, THE VILLAGE IS VULNERABLE! WE COULD MOUNT AN ATTACK IN FORCE AND ...
DZIIING
JUST LIKE THAT, RUNNING OVER THE GRASS? YUK, YUK AND YUK AGAIN!
NO, I HAVE A BETTER PLAN. WE'LL SEND FOR THAT SCROLL BY AIR MAIL!
EEK!
AND IN THE GAULISH VILLAGE ...
... AND SO IT WAS THAT I, VITALSTATISTIX, GAULISH CHIEFTAIN, GLORIOUSLY STOOD UP TO CAESAR'S ARMIES FOR YEARS ON END ...
HMM, YES ... ALL THANKS TO THE DRUID'S MAGIC POTION, DON'T FORGET!
25B

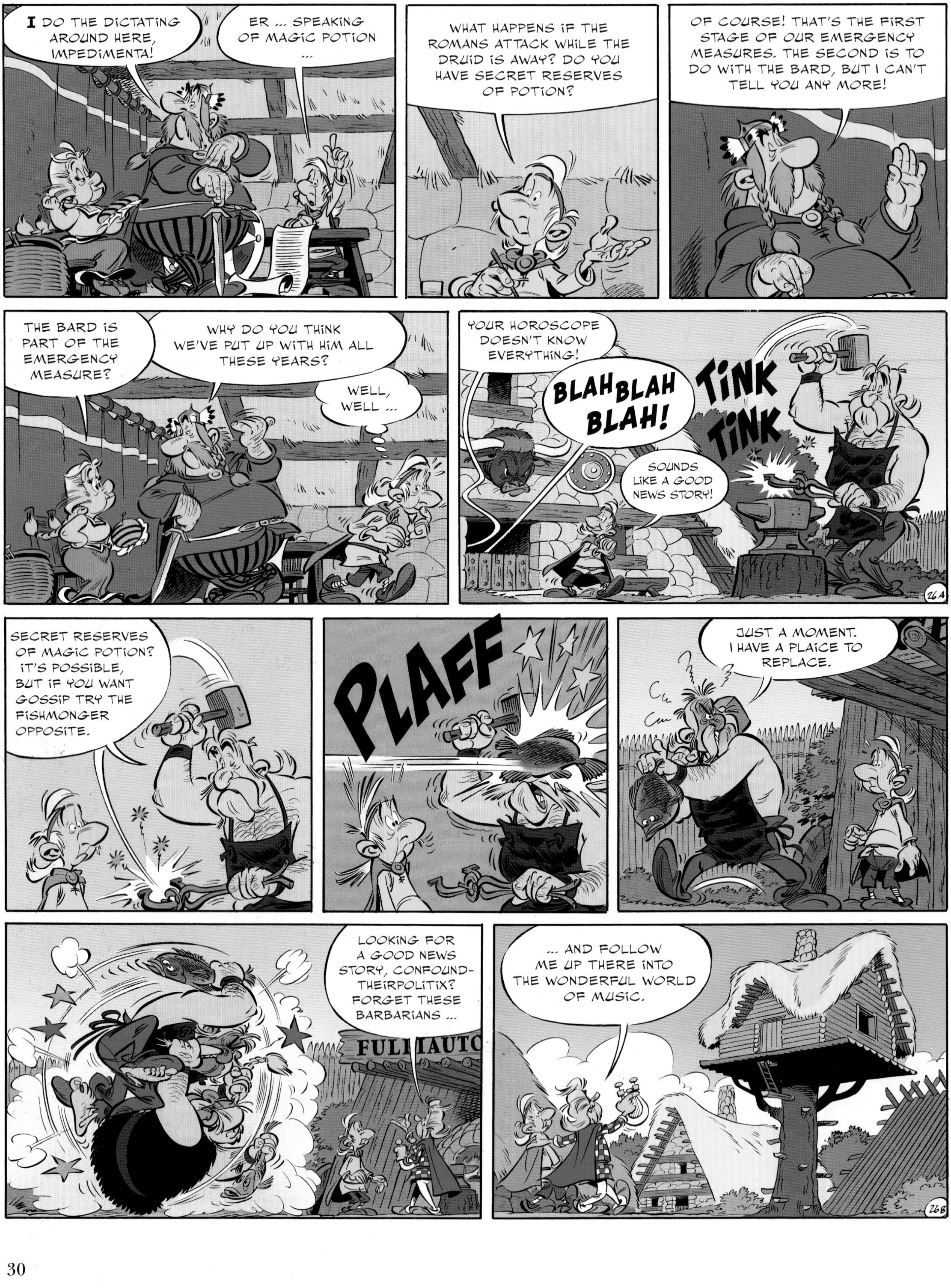
I DO THE DICTATING AROUND HERE, IMPEDIMENTA!
ER ... SPEAKING OF MAGIC POTION ...
WHAT HAPPENS IF THE ROMANS ATTACK WHILE THE DRUID IS AWAY? DO YOU HAVE SECRET RESERVES OF POTION?
OF COURSE! THAT'S THE FIRST STAGE OF OUR EMERGENCY MEASURES. THE SECOND IS TO DO WITH THE BARD, BUT I CAN'T TELL YOU ANY MORE!
THE BARD IS PART OF THE EMERGENCY MEASURE?
WHY DO YOU THINK WE'VE PUT UP WITH HIM ALL THESE YEARS?
WELL, WELL ...
YOUR HOROSCOPE DOESN'T KNOW EVERYTHING!
BLAH BLAH BLAH!
TINK TINK
SOUNDS LIKE A GOOD NEWS STORY!
SECRET RESERVES OF MAGIC POTION? IT'S POSSIBLE, BUT IF YOU WANT GOSSIP TRY THE FISHMONGER OPPOSITE.
PLAFF
JUST A MOMENT. I HAVE A PLAICE TO REPLACE.
LOOKING FOR A GOOD NEWS STORY, CONFOUND-THEIRPOLITIX? FORGET THESE BARBARIANS ...
... AND FOLLOW ME UP THERE INTO THE WONDERFUL WORLD OF MUSIC.

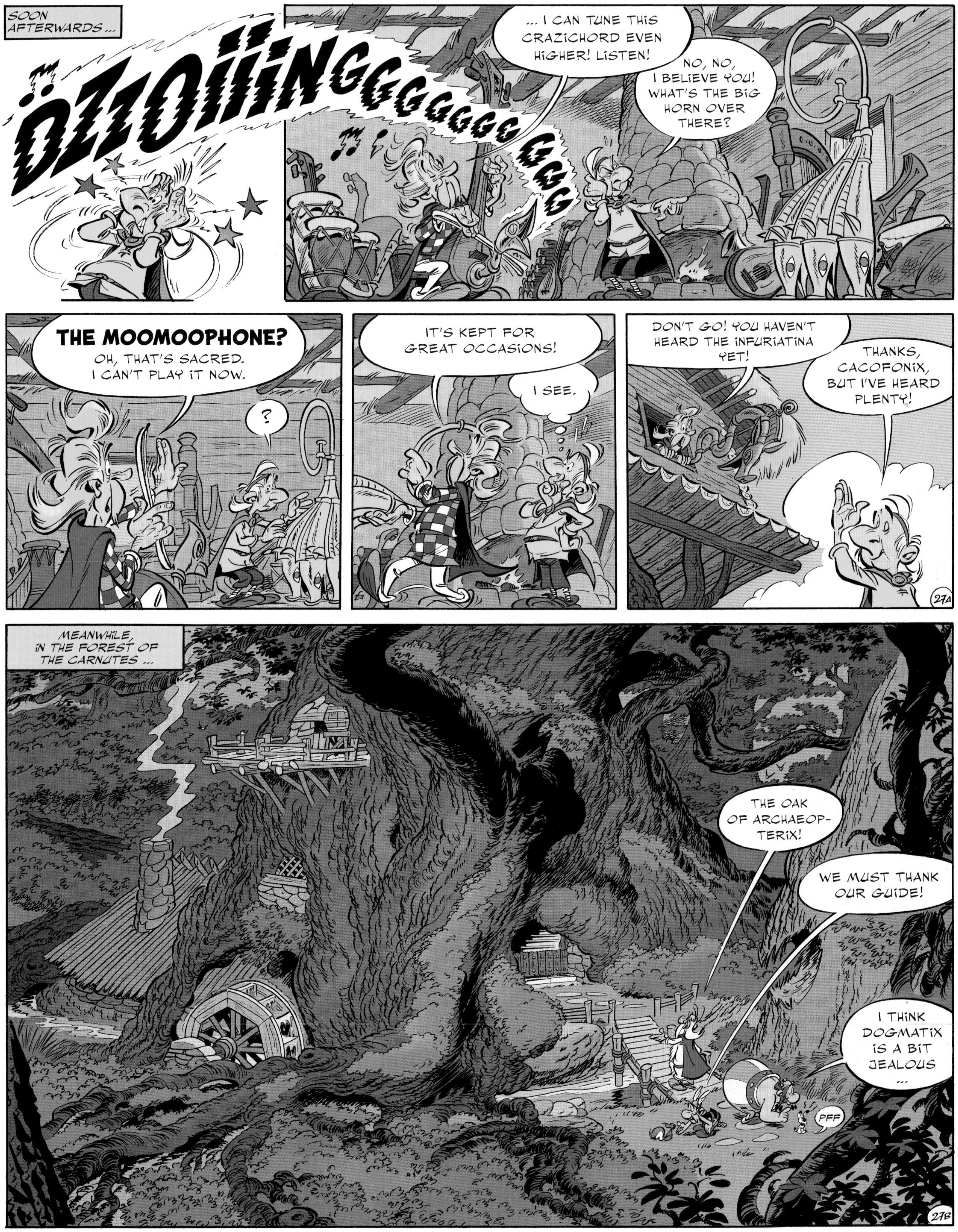
SOON AFTERWARDS ...
DZZOIIINGGGGGGGGGG
... I CAN TUNE THIS CRAZICHORD EVEN HIGHER! LISTEN!
NO, NO, I BELIEVE YOU! WHAT'S THE BIG HORN OVER THERE?
THE MOOMOOPHONE? OH, THAT'S SACRED. I CAN'T PLAY IT NOW.
?
IT'S KEPT FOR GREAT OCCASIONS!
I SEE.
DON'T GO! YOU HAVEN'T HEARD THE INFURIATINA YET!
THANKS, CACOFONIX, BUT I'VE HEARD PLENTY!
27A
MEANWHILE, IN THE FOREST OF THE CARNUTES ...
THE OAK OF ARCHAEOP-TERIX!
WE MUST THANK OUR GUIDE!
I THINK DOGMATIX IS A BIT JEALOUS ...
PFF
27B

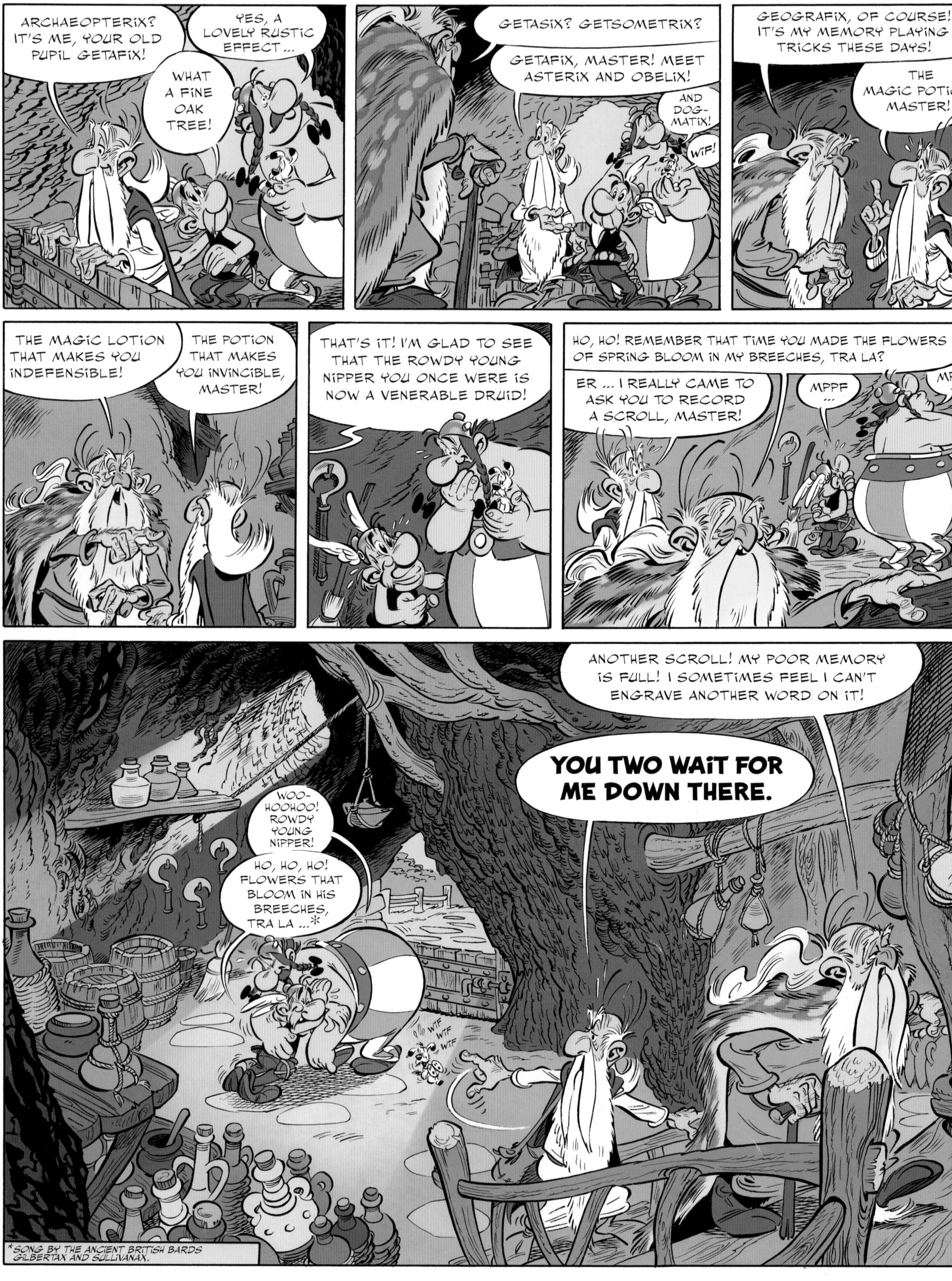
ARCHAEOPTERIX? IT'S ME, YOUR OLD PUPIL GETAFIX!
YES, A LOVELY RUSTIC EFFECT ...
WHAT A FINE OAK TREE!
GETASIX? GETSOMETRIX?
GETAFIX, MASTER! MEET ASTERIX AND OBELIX!
AND DOG-MATIX!
WIF!
GEOGRAFIX, OF COURSE! IT'S MY MEMORY PLAYING TRICKS THESE DAYS!
THE MAGIC POTION, MASTER!
THE MAGIC LOTION THAT MAKES YOU INDEFENSIBLE!
THE POTION THAT MAKES YOU INVINCIBLE, MASTER!
THAT'S IT! I'M GLAD TO SEE THAT THE ROWDY YOUNG NIPPER YOU ONCE WERE IS NOW A VENERABLE DRUID!
HO, HO! REMEMBER THAT TIME YOU MADE THE FLOWERS OF SPRING BLOOM IN MY BREECHES, TRA LA?
ER ... I REALLY CAME TO ASK YOU TO RECORD A SCROLL, MASTER!
MPPF ...
MPPF ...
28A
ANOTHER SCROLL! MY POOR MEMORY IS FULL! I SOMETIMES FEEL I CAN'T ENGRAVE ANOTHER WORD ON IT!
YOU TWO WAIT FOR ME DOWN THERE.
WOO-HOOHOO! ROWDY YOUNG NIPPER!
HO, HO, HO! FLOWERS THAT BLOOM IN HIS BREECHES, TRA LA ...*
WIF WIF WIF
*SONG BY THE ANCIENT BRITISH BARDS GILBERTAX AND SULLIVANAX.
28B

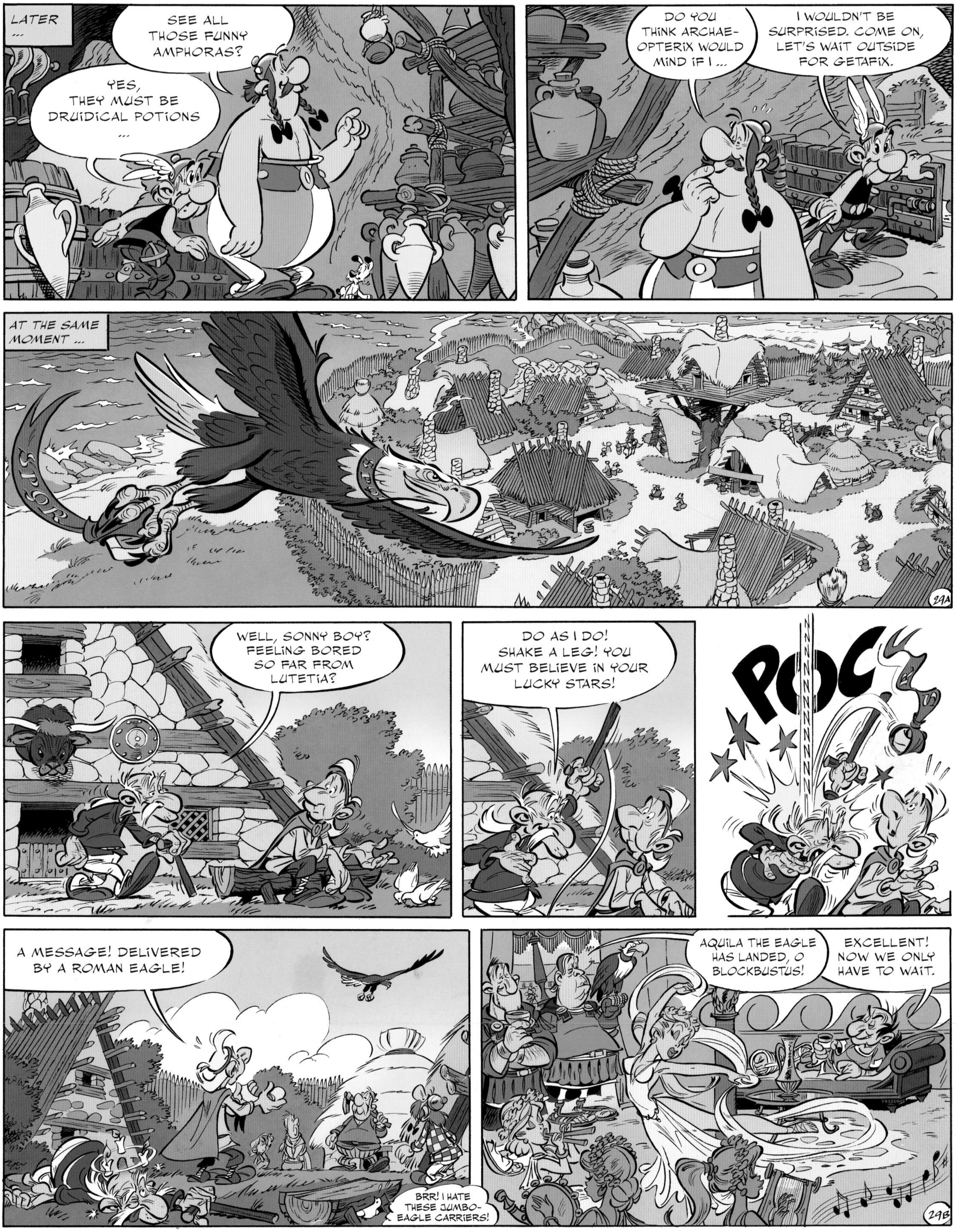
LATER ...
SEE ALL THOSE FUNNY AMPHORAS?
YES, THEY MUST BE DRUIDICAL POTIONS ...
DO YOU THINK ARCHAEOPTERIX WOULD MIND IF I ...
I WOULDN'T BE SURPRISED. COME ON, LET'S WAIT OUTSIDE FOR GETAFIX.
AT THE SAME MOMENT ...
SPQR
29A
WELL, SONNY BOY? FEELING BORED SO FAR FROM LUTETIA?
DO AS I DO! SHAKE A LEG! YOU MUST BELIEVE IN YOUR LUCKY STARS!
POC
A MESSAGE! DELIVERED BY A ROMAN EAGLE!
BRR! I HATE THESE JUMBO-EAGLE CARRIERS!
AQUILA THE EAGLE HAS LANDED, O BLOCKBUSTUS!
EXCELLENT! NOW WE ONLY HAVE TO WAIT.
29B

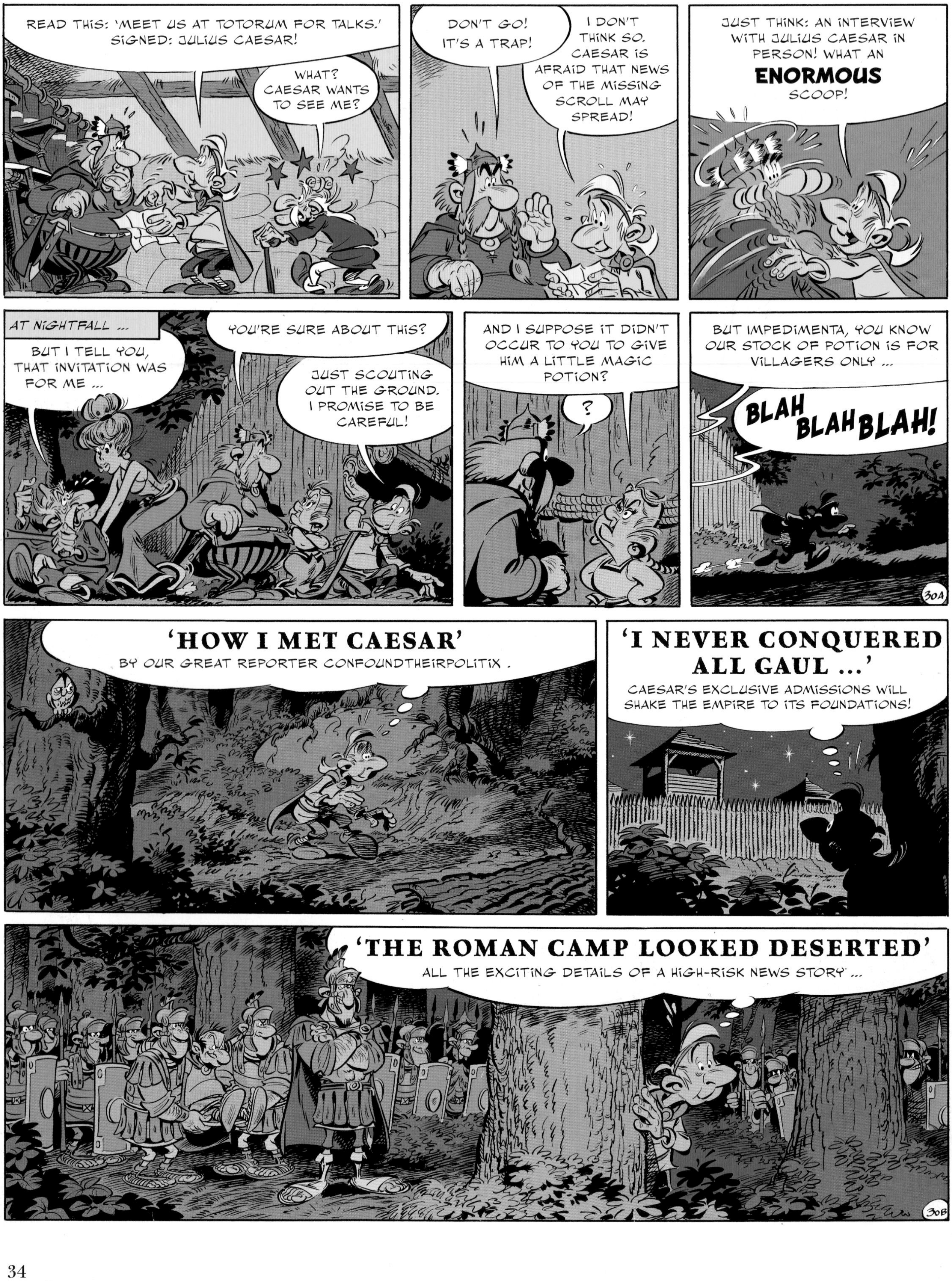
READ THIS: 'MEET US AT TOTORUM FOR TALKS.' SIGNED: JULIUS CAESAR!
WHAT? CAESAR WANTS TO SEE ME?
DON'T GO! IT'S A TRAP!
I DON'T THINK SO. CAESAR IS AFRAID THAT NEWS OF THE MISSING SCROLL MAY SPREAD!
JUST THINK: AN INTERVIEW WITH JULIUS CAESAR IN PERSON! WHAT AN ENORMOUS SCOOP!
AT NIGHTFALL ...
BUT I TELL YOU, THAT INVITATION WAS FOR ME ...
YOU'RE SURE ABOUT THIS?
JUST SCOUTING OUT THE GROUND. I PROMISE TO BE CAREFUL!
AND I SUPPOSE IT DIDN'T OCCUR TO YOU TO GIVE HIM A LITTLE MAGIC POTION?
?
BUT IMPEDIMENTA, YOU KNOW OUR STOCK OF POTION IS FOR VILLAGERS ONLY ...
BLAH BLAH BLAH!
30A
'HOW I MET CAESAR'
BY OUR GREAT REPORTER CONFOUNDTHEIRPOLITIX.
'I NEVER CONQUERED ALL GAUL ...'
CAESAR'S EXCLUSIVE ADMISSIONS WILL SHAKE THE EMPIRE TO ITS FOUNDATIONS!
'THE ROMAN CAMP LOOKED DESERTED'
ALL THE EXCITING DETAILS OF A HIGH-RISK NEWS STORY ...
30B

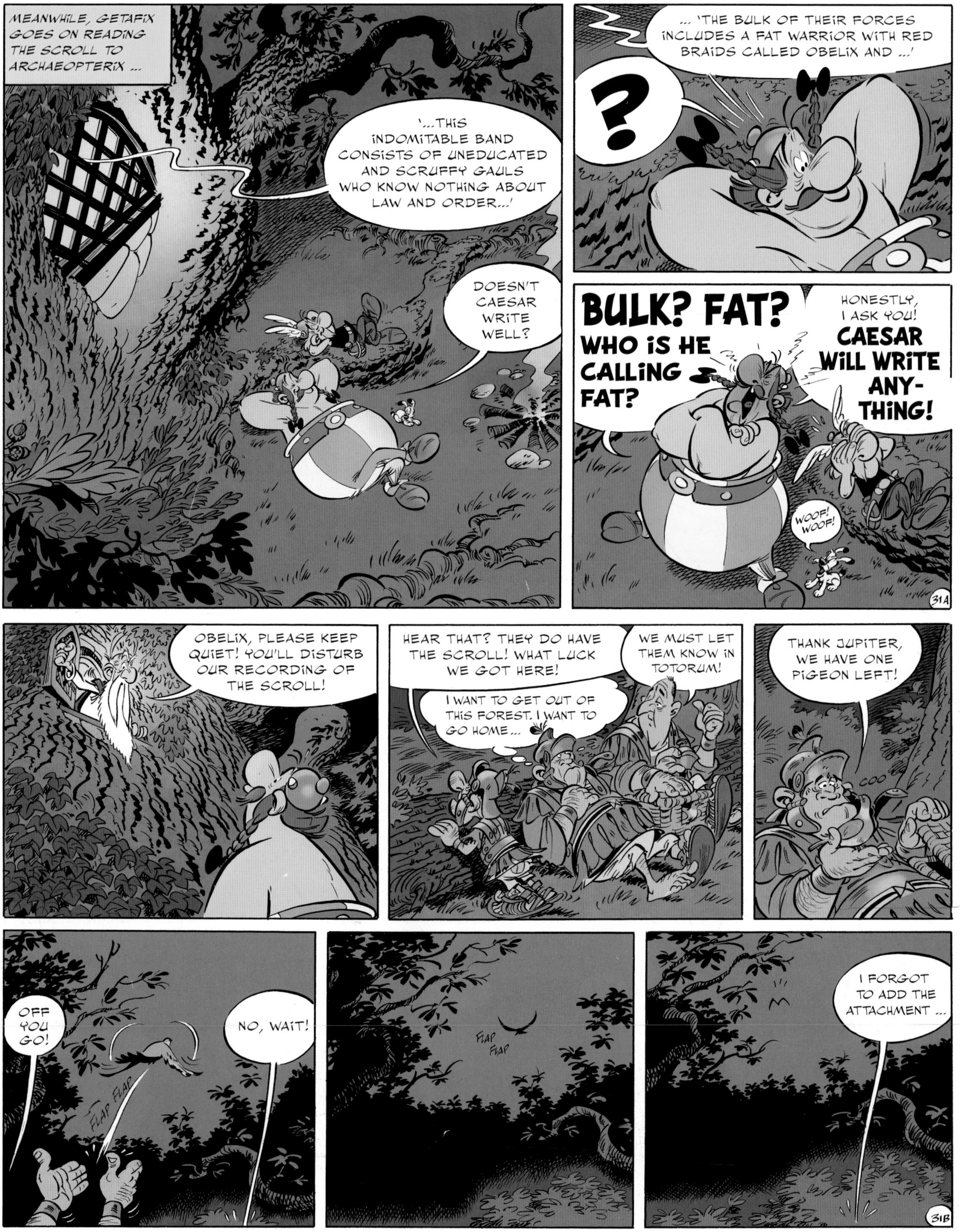
MEANWHILE, GETAFIX GOES ON READING THE SCROLL TO ARCHAEOPTERIX ...
'...THIS INDOMITABLE BAND CONSISTS OF UNEDUCATED AND SCRUFFY GAULS WHO KNOW NOTHING ABOUT LAW AND ORDER...'
DOESN'T CAESAR WRITE WELL?
... 'THE BULK OF THEIR FORCES INCLUDES A FAT WARRIOR WITH RED BRAIDS CALLED OBELIX AND ...'
?
BULK? FAT? WHO IS HE CALLING FAT?
HONESTLY, I ASK YOU! CAESAR WILL WRITE ANY-THING!
WOOF! WOOF!
31A
OBELIX, PLEASE KEEP QUIET! YOU'LL DISTURB OUR RECORDING OF THE SCROLL!
HEAR THAT? THEY DO HAVE THE SCROLL! WHAT LUCK WE GOT HERE!
WE MUST LET THEM KNOW IN TOTORUM!
I WANT TO GET OUT OF THIS FOREST. I WANT TO GO HOME ...
THANK JUPITER, WE HAVE ONE PIGEON LEFT!
COO
OFF YOU GO!
NO, WAIT!
FLAP FLAP
FLAP FLAP
I FORGOT TO ADD THE ATTACHMENT ...
31B

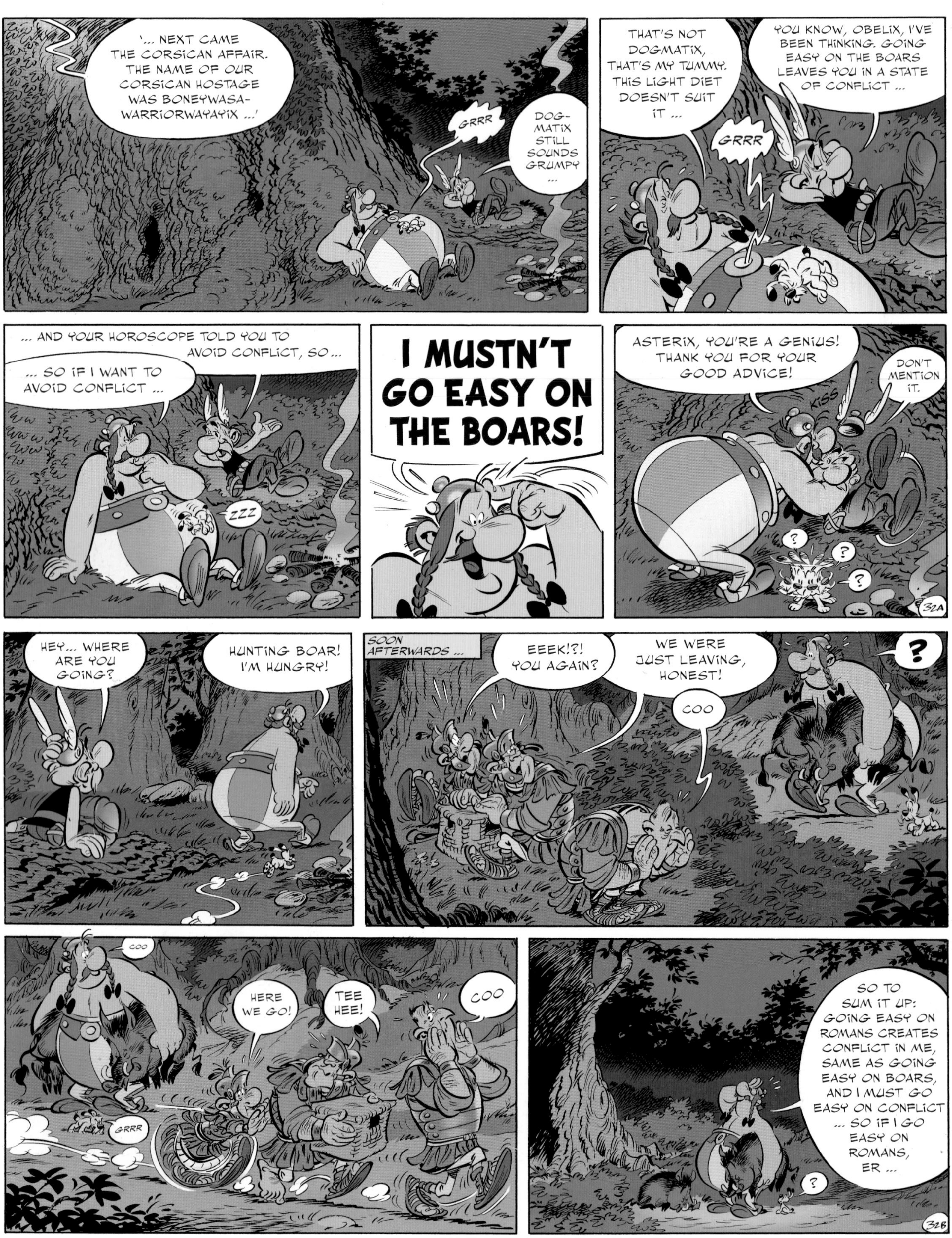
'... NEXT CAME THE CORSICAN AFFAIR. THE NAME OF OUR CORSICAN HOSTAGE WAS BONEYWASA-WARRIORWAYAYIX ...'
GRRR
DOG-MATIX STILL SOUNDS GRUMPY ...
THAT'S NOT DOGMATIX, THAT'S MY TUMMY. THIS LIGHT DIET DOESN'T SUIT IT ...
YOU KNOW, OBELIX, I'VE BEEN THINKING. GOING EASY ON THE BOARS LEAVES YOU IN A STATE OF CONFLICT ...
GRRR
... AND YOUR HOROSCOPE TOLD YOU TO AVOID CONFLICT, SO ...
... SO IF I WANT TO AVOID CONFLICT ...
ZZZ
I MUSTN'T GO EASY ON THE BOARS!
ASTERIX, YOU'RE A GENIUS! THANK YOU FOR YOUR GOOD ADVICE!
DON'T MENTION IT.
KISS
HEY... WHERE ARE YOU GOING?
HUNTING BOAR! I'M HUNGRY!
SOON AFTERWARDS ...
EEEK!?! YOU AGAIN?
WE WERE JUST LEAVING, HONEST!
COO
?
COO
HERE WE GO!
TEE HEE!
COO
GRRR
SO TO SUM IT UP: GOING EASY ON ROMANS CREATES CONFLICT IN ME, SAME AS GOING EASY ON BOARS, AND I MUST GO EASY ON CONFLICT ... SO IF I GO EASY ON ROMANS, ER ...
?

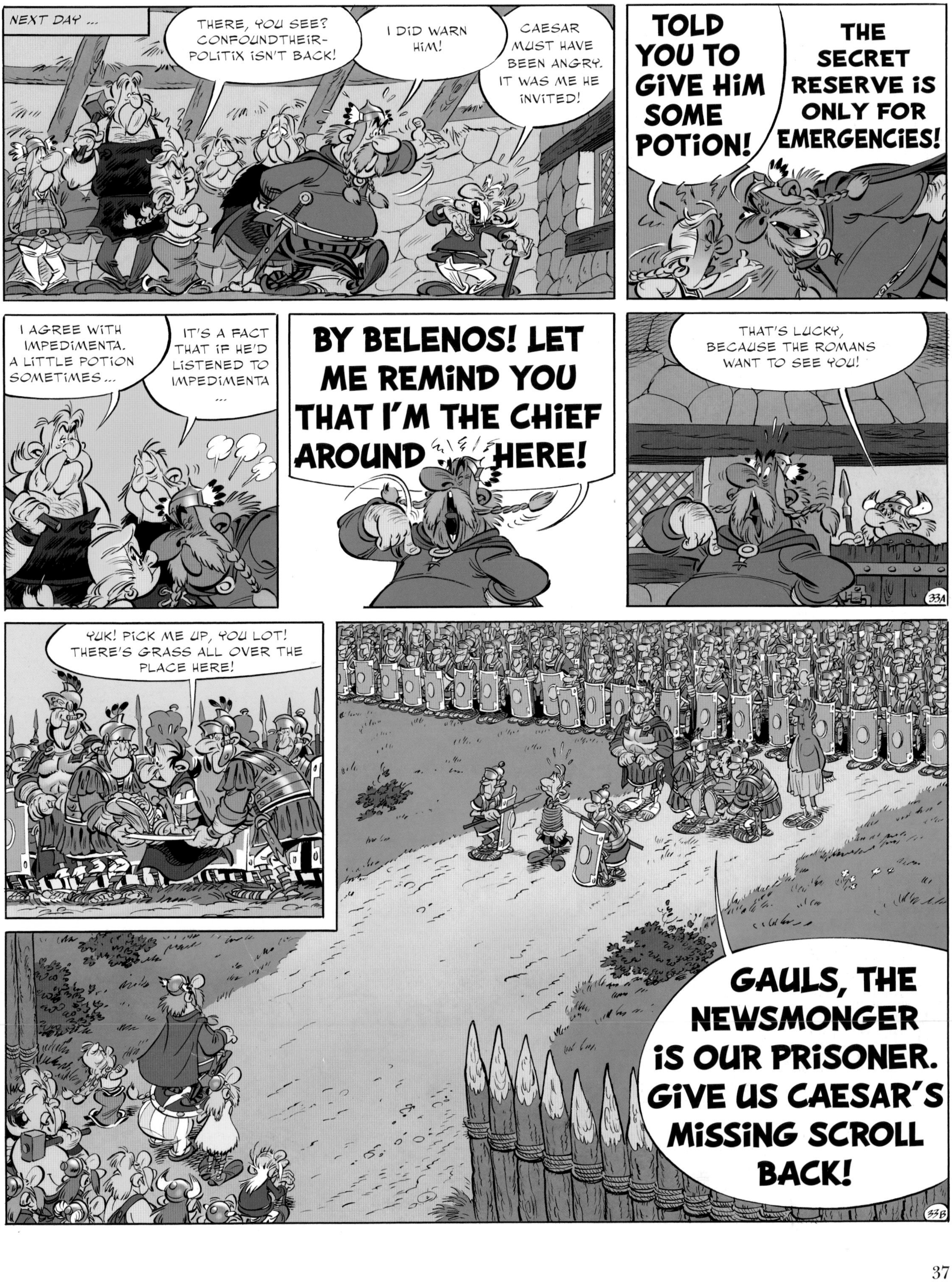
NEXT DAY ...
THERE, YOU SEE? CONFOUNDTHEIR-POLITIX ISN'T BACK!
I DID WARN HIM!
CAESAR MUST HAVE BEEN ANGRY. IT WAS ME HE INVITED!
TOLD YOU TO GIVE HIM SOME POTION!
THE SECRET RESERVE IS ONLY FOR EMERGENCIES!
I AGREE WITH IMPEDIMENTA. A LITTLE POTION SOMETIMES ...
IT'S A FACT THAT IF HE'D LISTENED TO IMPEDIMENTA ...
BY BELENOS! LET ME REMIND YOU THAT I'M THE CHIEF AROUND HERE!
THAT'S LUCKY, BECAUSE THE ROMANS WANT TO SEE YOU!
33A
YUK! PICK ME UP, YOU LOT! THERE'S GRASS ALL OVER THE PLACE HERE!
GAULS, THE NEWSMONGER IS OUR PRISONER. GIVE US CAESAR'S MISSING SCROLL BACK!
33B

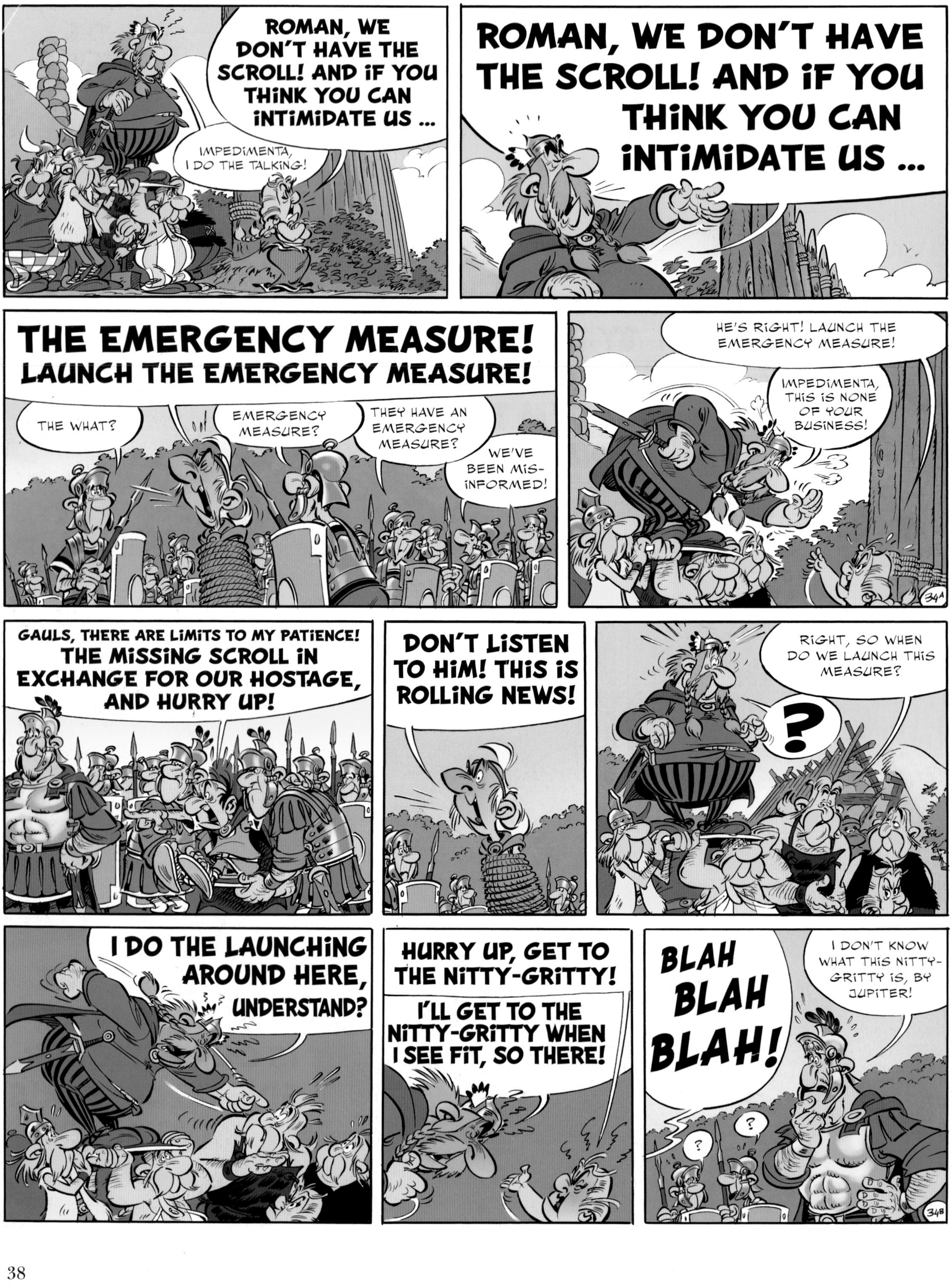
ROMAN, WE DON'T HAVE THE SCROLL! AND IF YOU THINK YOU CAN INTIMIDATE US ...
IMPEDIMENTA, I DO THE TALKING!
ROMAN, WE DON'T HAVE THE SCROLL! AND IF YOU THINK YOU CAN INTIMIDATE US ...
THE EMERGENCY MEASURE! LAUNCH THE EMERGENCY MEASURE!
THE WHAT?
EMERGENCY MEASURE?
THEY HAVE AN EMERGENCY MEASURE?
WE'VE BEEN MIS-INFORMED!
HE'S RIGHT! LAUNCH THE EMERGENCY MEASURE!
IMPEDIMENTA, THIS IS NONE OF YOUR BUSINESS!
34A
GAULS, THERE ARE LIMITS TO MY PATIENCE! THE MISSING SCROLL IN EXCHANGE FOR OUR HOSTAGE, AND HURRY UP!
DON'T LISTEN TO HIM! THIS IS ROLLING NEWS!
RIGHT, SO WHEN DO WE LAUNCH THIS MEASURE?
?
I DO THE LAUNCHING AROUND HERE, UNDERSTAND?
HURRY UP, GET TO THE NITTY-GRITTY!
I'LL GET TO THE NITTY-GRITTY WHEN I SEE FIT, SO THERE!
BLAH BLAH BLAH!
I DON'T KNOW WHAT THIS NITTY-GRITTY IS, BY JUPITER!
34B

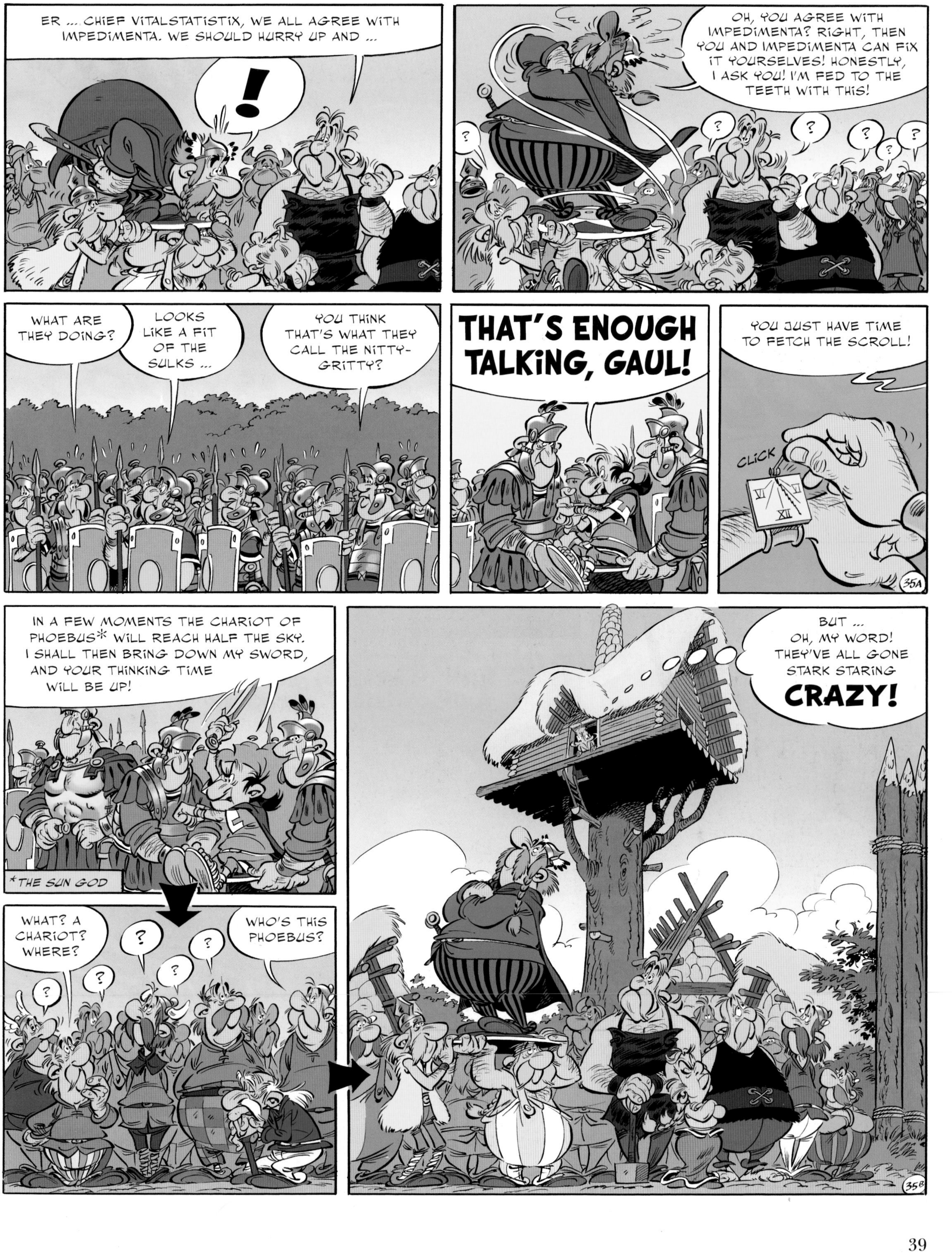
ER ... CHIEF VITALSTATISTIX, WE ALL AGREE WITH IMPEDIMENTA. WE SHOULD HURRY UP AND ...
!
OH, YOU AGREE WITH IMPEDIMENTA? RIGHT, THEN YOU AND IMPEDIMENTA CAN FIX IT YOURSELVES! HONESTLY, I ASK YOU! I'M FED TO THE TEETH WITH THIS!
?
?
?
?
?
?
WHAT ARE THEY DOING?
LOOKS LIKE A FIT OF THE SULKS ...
YOU THINK THAT'S WHAT THEY CALL THE NITTY-GRITTY?
THAT'S ENOUGH TALKING, GAUL!
YOU JUST HAVE TIME TO FETCH THE SCROLL!
CLICK
IN A FEW MOMENTS THE CHARIOT OF PHOEBUS* WILL REACH HALF THE SKY. I SHALL THEN BRING DOWN MY SWORD, AND YOUR THINKING TIME WILL BE UP!
*THE SUN GOD
WHAT? A CHARIOT? WHERE?
?
?
?
?
?
WHO'S THIS PHOEBUS?
BUT ... OH, MY WORD! THEY'VE ALL GONE STARK STARING CRAZY!

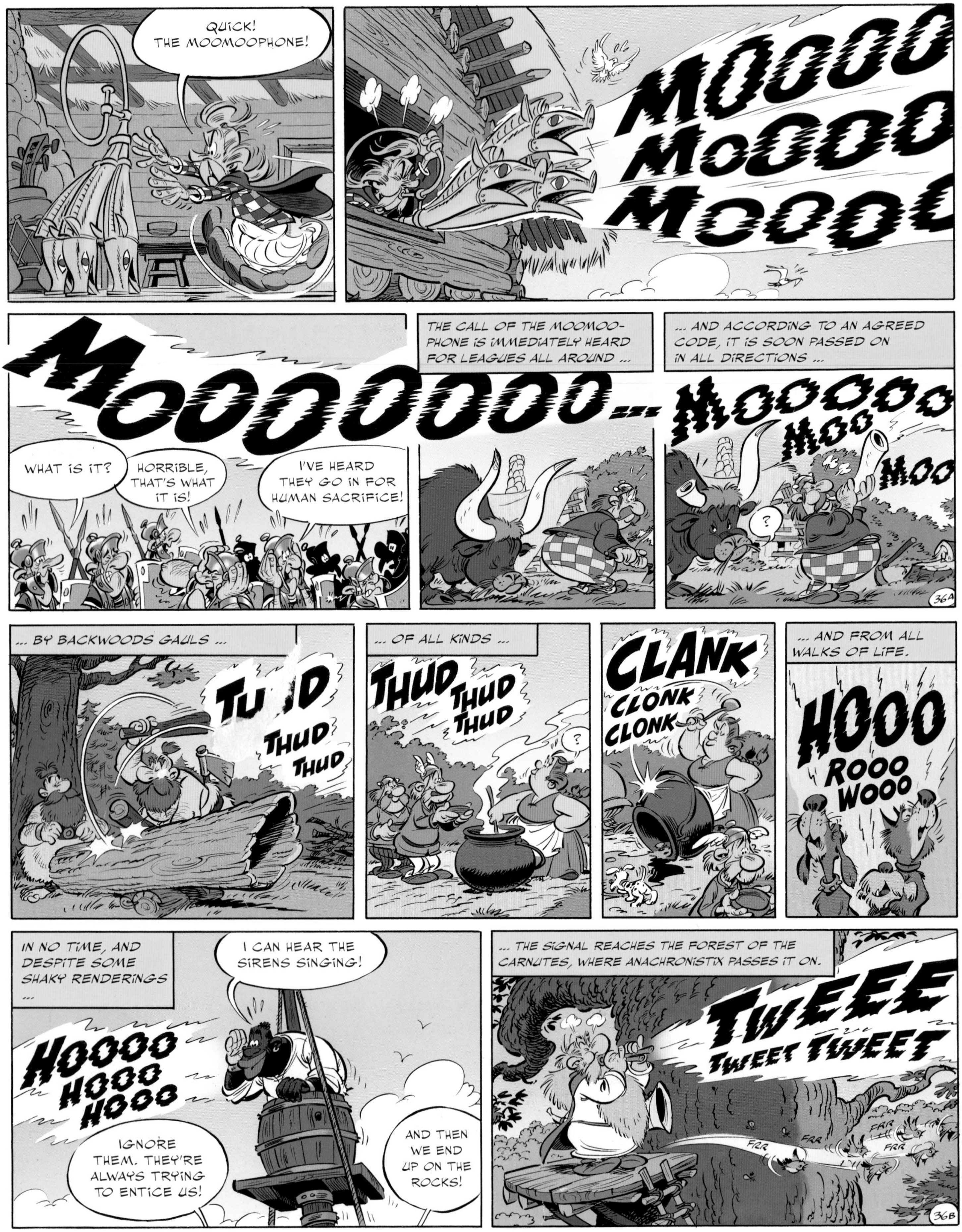
QUICK! THE MOOMOOPHONE!
MOOOOO MOOOOO MOOOOO
MOOOOOOOO...
WHAT IS IT?
HORRIBLE, THAT'S WHAT IT IS!
I'VE HEARD THEY GO IN FOR HUMAN SACRIFICE!
THE CALL OF THE MOOMOO-PHONE IS IMMEDIATELY HEARD FOR LEAGUES ALL AROUND ...
... AND ACCORDING TO AN AGREED CODE, IT IS SOON PASSED ON IN ALL DIRECTIONS ...
MOOOOO MOO MOO
?
36A
... BY BACKWOODS GAULS ...
THUD THUD THUD
... OF ALL KINDS ...
THUD THUD THUD
?
CLANK CLONK CLONK
... AND FROM ALL WALKS OF LIFE.
HOOO ROOO WOOO
IN NO TIME, AND DESPITE SOME SHAKY RENDERINGS ...
I CAN HEAR THE SIRENS SINGING!
HOOOO HOOO HOOO
IGNORE THEM. THEY'RE ALWAYS TRYING TO ENTICE US!
AND THEN WE END UP ON THE ROCKS!
... THE SIGNAL REACHES THE FOREST OF THE CARNUTES, WHERE ANACHRONISTIX PASSES IT ON.
TWEEE TWEET TWEET
FRR FRR FRR FRR
36B

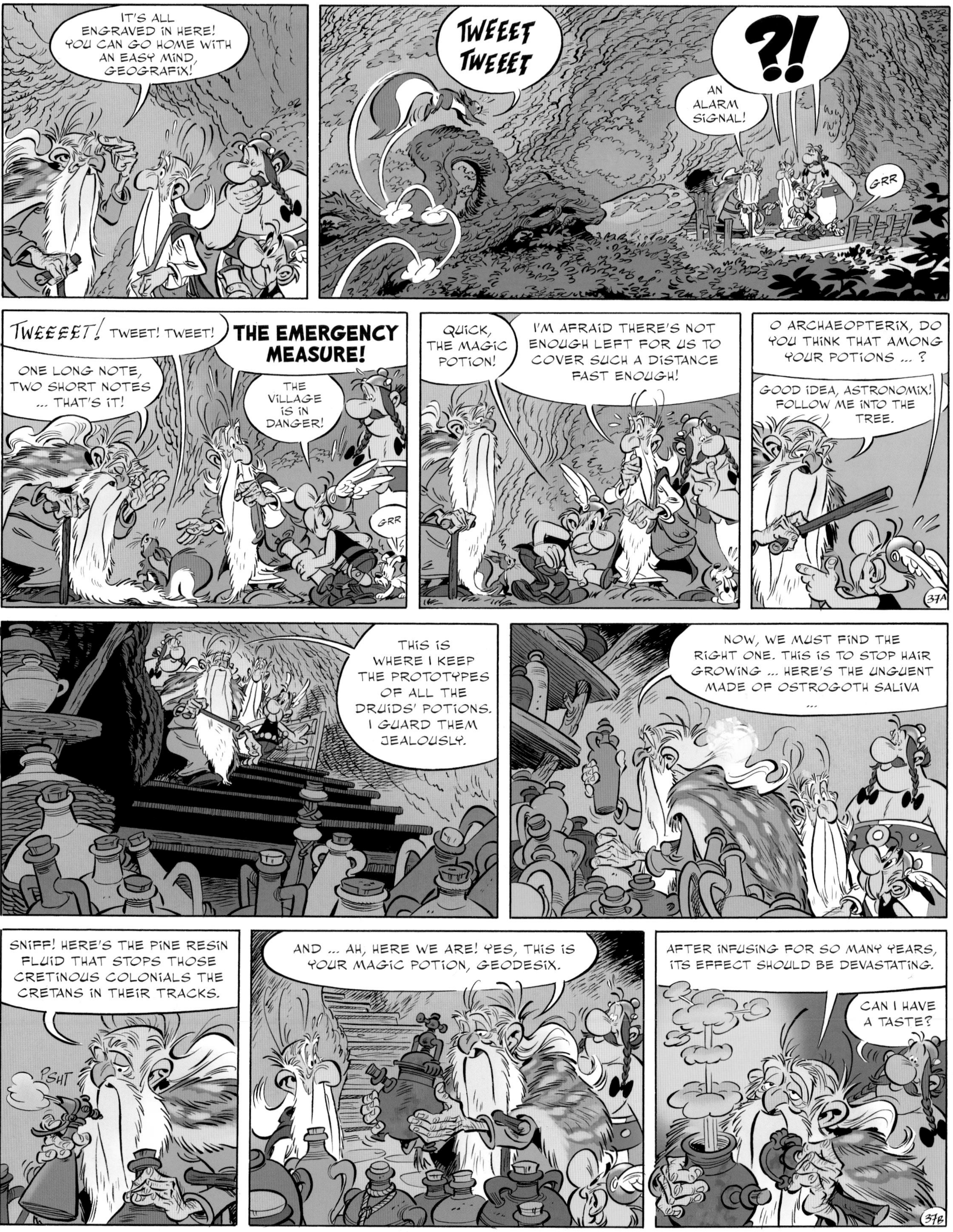

IT'S ALL ENGRAVED IN HERE! YOU CAN GO HOME WITH AN EASY MIND, GEOGRAFIX!
TWEEET TWEEET
?!
AN ALARM SIGNAL!
GRR
TWEEEET! TWEET! TWEET!
ONE LONG NOTE, TWO SHORT NOTES ... THAT'S IT!
THE EMERGENCY MEASURE!
THE VILLAGE IS IN DANGER!
GRR
QUICK, THE MAGIC POTION!
I'M AFRAID THERE'S NOT ENOUGH LEFT FOR US TO COVER SUCH A DISTANCE FAST ENOUGH!
O ARCHAEOPTERIX, DO YOU THINK THAT AMONG YOUR POTIONS ... ?
GOOD IDEA, ASTRONOMIX! FOLLOW ME INTO THE TREE.
THIS IS WHERE I KEEP THE PROTOTYPES OF ALL THE DRUIDS' POTIONS. I GUARD THEM JEALOUSLY.
NOW, WE MUST FIND THE RIGHT ONE. THIS IS TO STOP HAIR GROWING ... HERE'S THE UNGUENT MADE OF OSTROGOTH SALIVA ...
SNIFF! HERE'S THE PINE RESIN FLUID THAT STOPS THOSE CRETINOUS COLONIALS THE CRETANS IN THEIR TRACKS.
PSHT
AND ... AH, HERE WE ARE! YES, THIS IS YOUR MAGIC POTION, GEODESIX.
AFTER INFUSING FOR SO MANY YEARS, ITS EFFECT SHOULD BE DEVASTATING.
CAN I HAVE A TASTE?

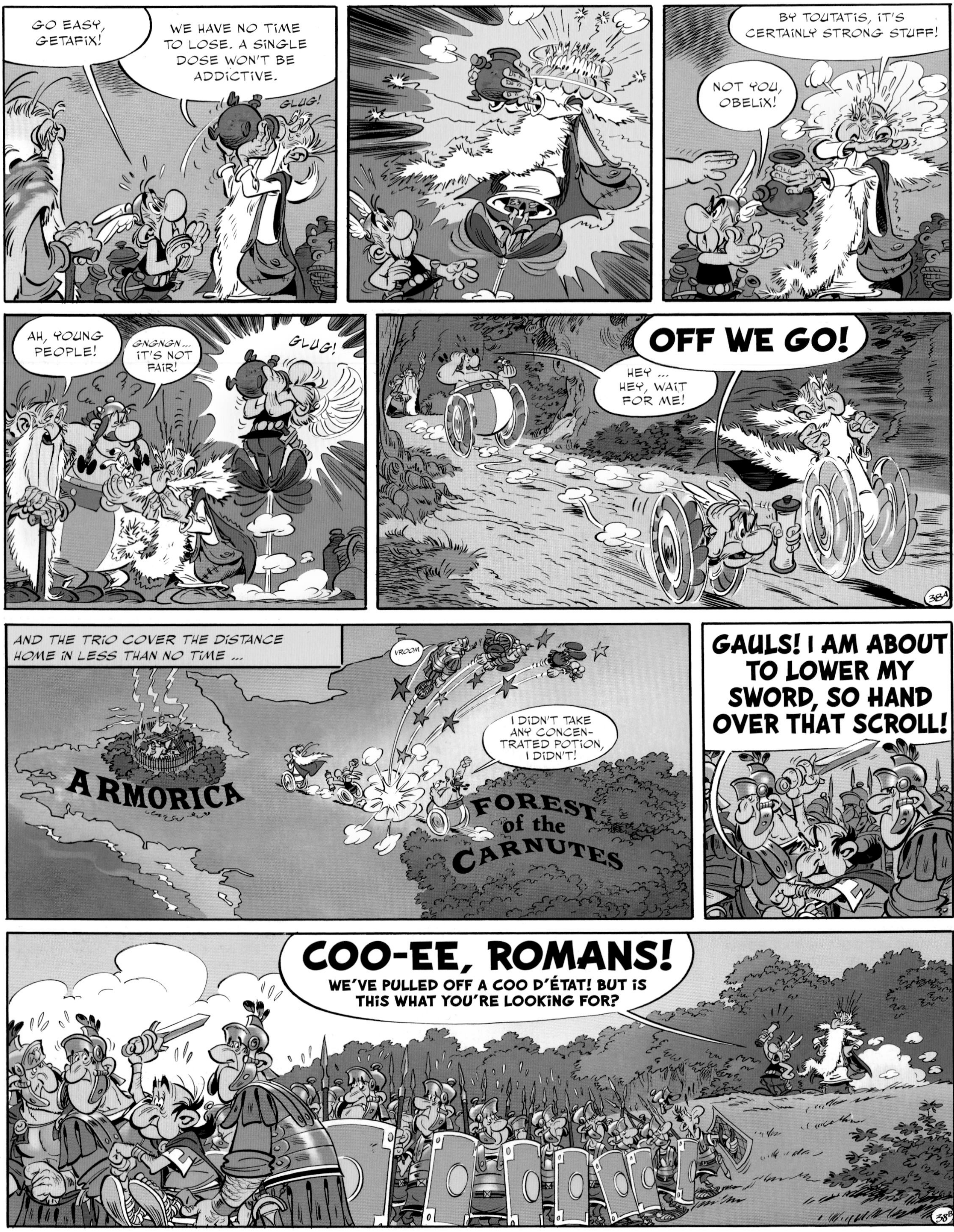
GO EASY, GETAFIX!
WE HAVE NO TIME TO LOSE. A SINGLE DOSE WON'T BE ADDICTIVE.
GLUG!
BY TOUTATIS, IT'S CERTAINLY STRONG STUFF!
NOT YOU, OBELIX!
AH, YOUNG PEOPLE!
GNGNGN... IT'S NOT FAIR!
GLUG!
OFF WE GO!
HEY ... HEY, WAIT FOR ME!
38A
AND THE TRIO COVER THE DISTANCE HOME IN LESS THAN NO TIME ...
VROOM
I DIDN'T TAKE ANY CONCEN-TRATED POTION, I DIDN'T!
ARMORICA
FOREST of the CARNUTES
GAULS! I AM ABOUT TO LOWER MY SWORD, SO HAND OVER THAT SCROLL!
COO-EE, ROMANS!
WE'VE PULLED OFF A COO D'ÉTAT! BUT IS THIS WHAT YOU'RE LOOKING FOR?
38B

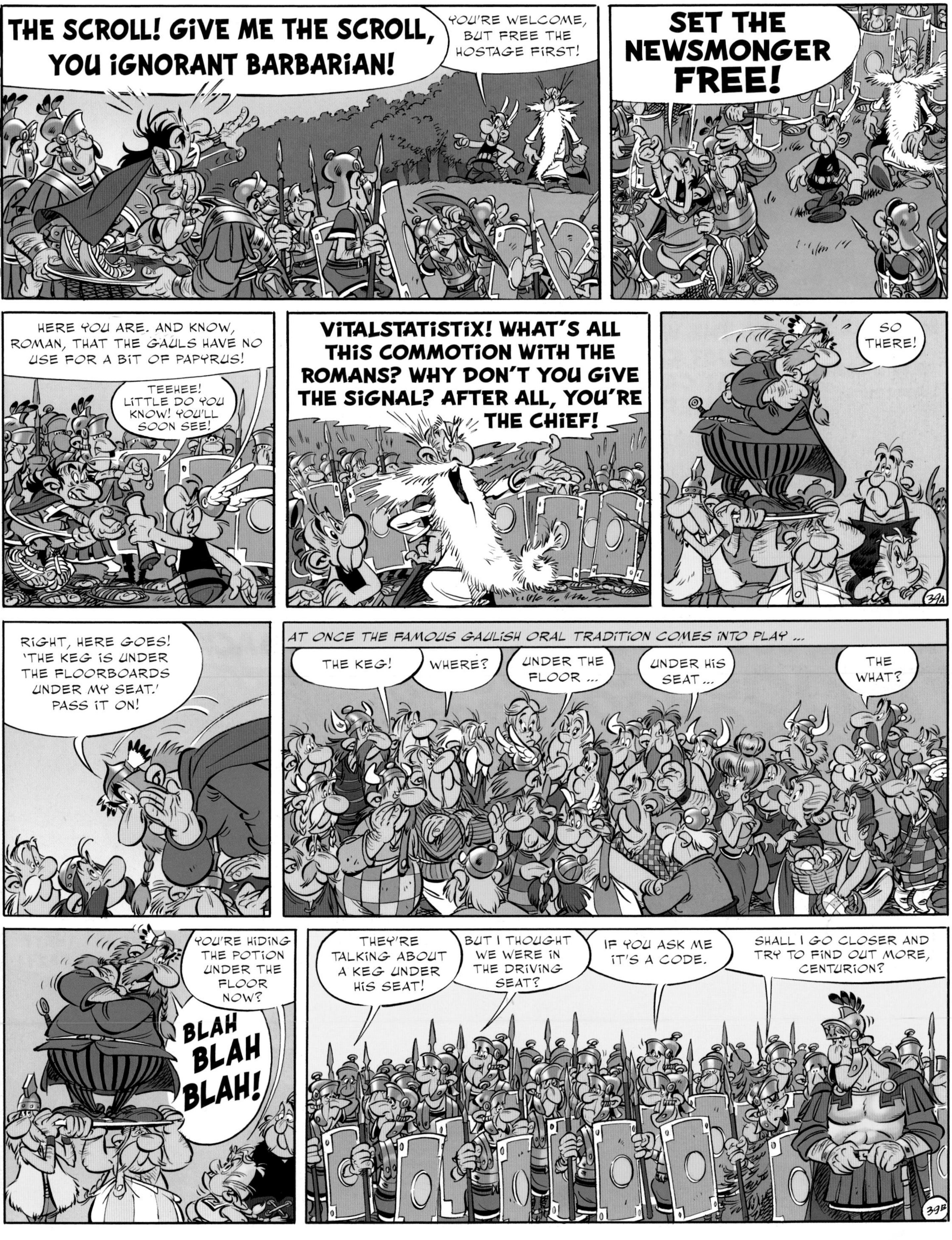
THE SCROLL! GiVE ME THE SCROLL, YOU iGNORANT BARBARiAN!
YOU'RE WELCOME, BUT FREE THE HOSTAGE FIRST!
SET THE NEWSMONGER FREE!
HERE YOU ARE. AND KNOW, ROMAN, THAT THE GAULS HAVE NO USE FOR A BIT OF PAPYRUS!
TEEHEE! LITTLE DO YOU KNOW! YOU'LL SOON SEE!
ViTALSTATiSTiX! WHAT'S ALL THiS COMMOTiON WiTH THE ROMANS? WHY DON'T YOU GiVE THE SiGNAL? AFTER ALL, YOU'RE THE CHiEF!
SO THERE!
39A
RiGHT, HERE GOES! 'THE KEG iS UNDER THE FLOORBOARDS UNDER MY SEAT.' PASS iT ON!
AT ONCE THE FAMOUS GAULiSH ORAL TRADiTiON COMES iNTO PLAY ...
THE KEG!
WHERE?
UNDER THE FLOOR ...
UNDER HiS SEAT ...
THE WHAT?
YOU'RE HiDiNG THE POTiON UNDER THE FLOOR NOW?
BLAH BLAH BLAH!
THEY'RE TALKiNG ABOUT A KEG UNDER HiS SEAT!
BUT I THOUGHT WE WERE iN THE DRiViNG SEAT?
iF YOU ASK ME iT'S A CODE.
SHALL I GO CLOSER AND TRY TO FiND OUT MORE, CENTURiON?
39B

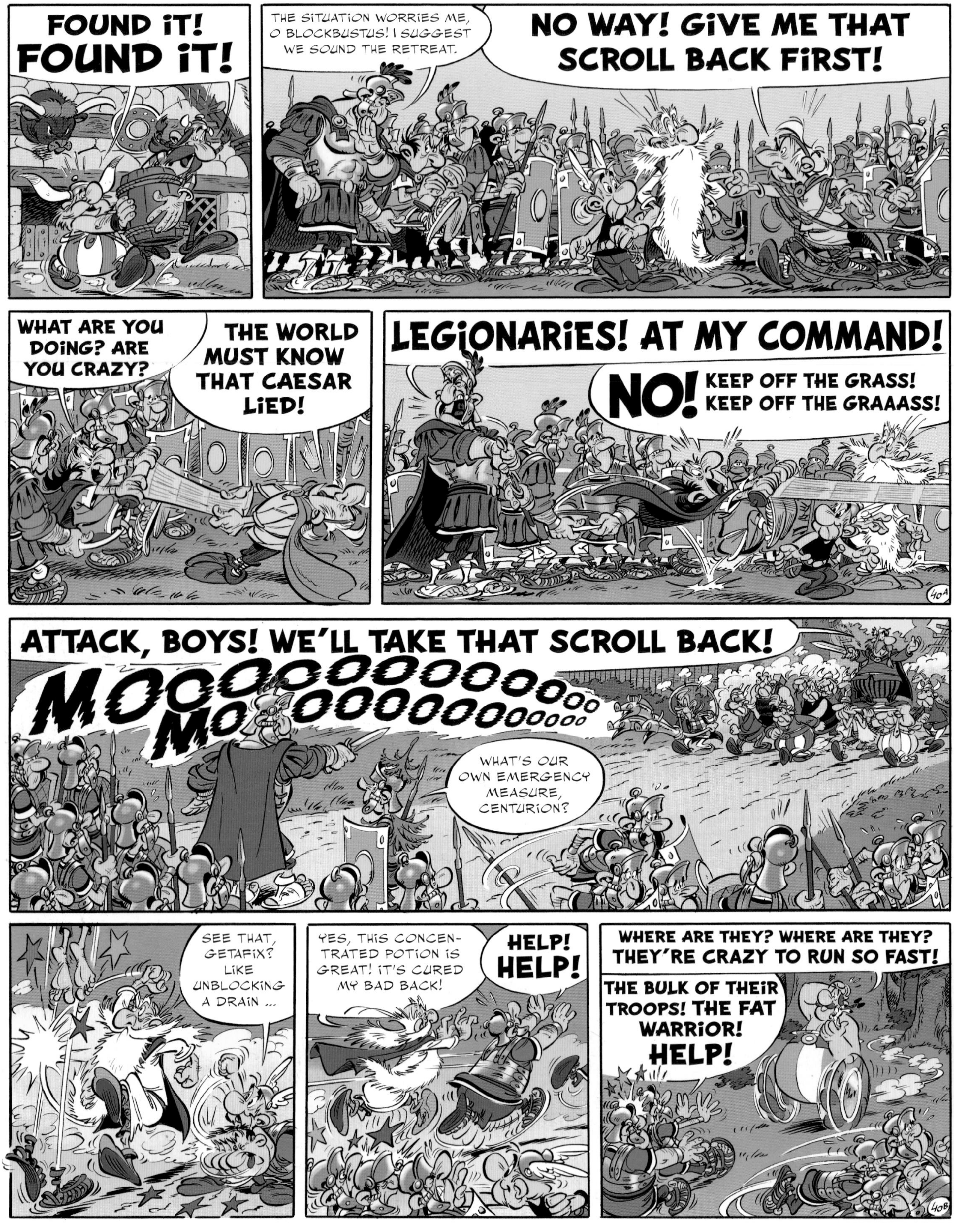
FOUND IT! FOUND IT!
THE SITUATION WORRIES ME, O BLOCKBUSTUS! I SUGGEST WE SOUND THE RETREAT.
NO WAY! GIVE ME THAT SCROLL BACK FIRST!
WHAT ARE YOU DOING? ARE YOU CRAZY?
THE WORLD MUST KNOW THAT CAESAR LIED!
LEGIONARIES! AT MY COMMAND!
NO! KEEP OFF THE GRASS! KEEP OFF THE GRAAASS!
40A
ATTACK, BOYS! WE'LL TAKE THAT SCROLL BACK!
MOOOOOOOOOOOooo
MOOOOOOOOOOOOooo
WHAT'S OUR OWN EMERGENCY MEASURE, CENTURION?
SEE THAT, GETAFIX? LIKE UNBLOCKING A DRAIN ...
YES, THIS CONCENTRATED POTION IS GREAT! IT'S CURED MY BAD BACK!
HELP! HELP!
WHERE ARE THEY? WHERE ARE THEY? THEY'RE CRAZY TO RUN SO FAST!
THE BULK OF THEIR TROOPS! THE FAT WARRIOR! HELP!
40B

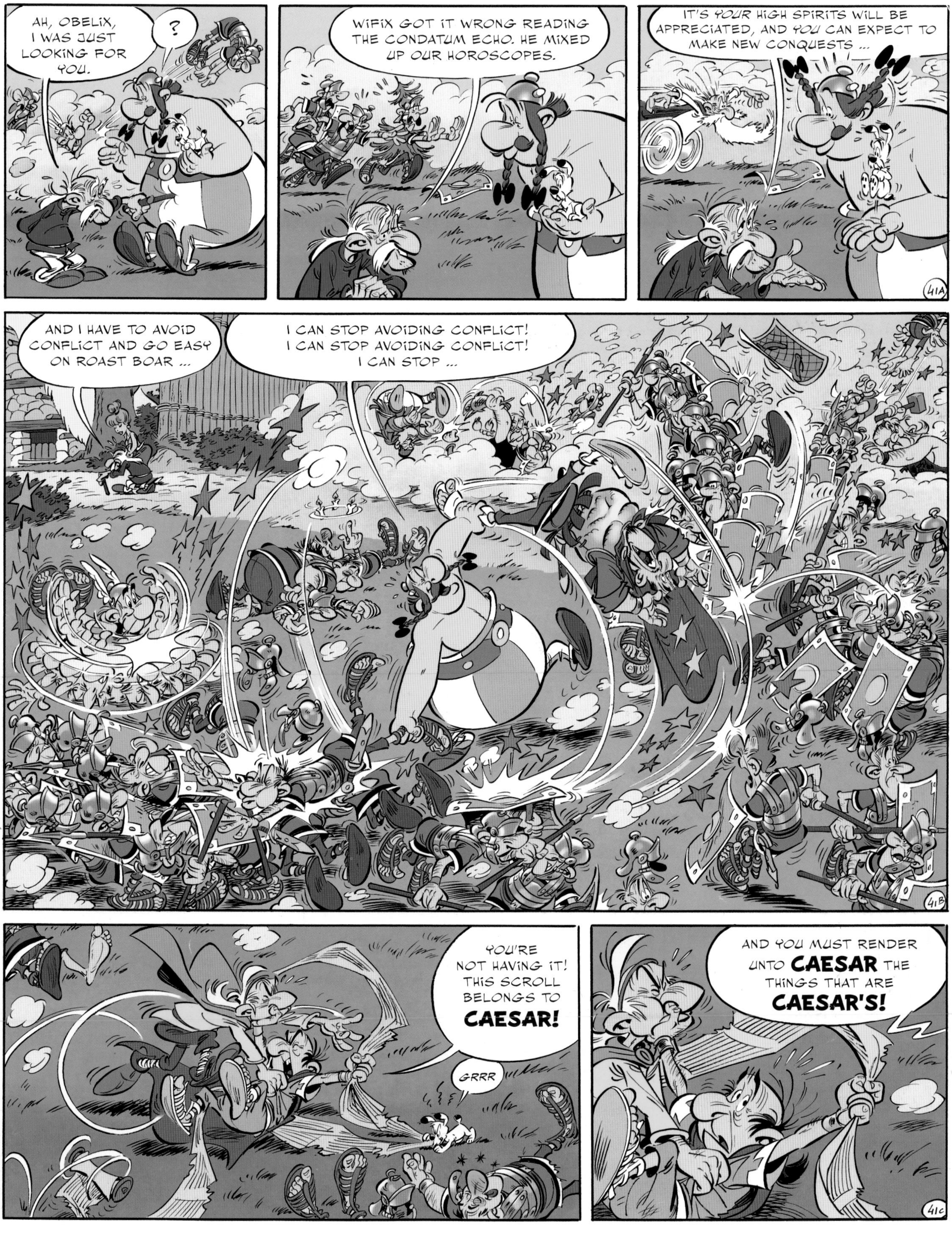
AH, OBELIX, I WAS JUST LOOKING FOR YOU.
?
WIFIX GOT IT WRONG READING THE CONDATUM ECHO. HE MIXED UP OUR HOROSCOPES.
IT'S YOUR HIGH SPIRITS WILL BE APPRECIATED, AND YOU CAN EXPECT TO MAKE NEW CONQUESTS ...
41A
AND I HAVE TO AVOID CONFLICT AND GO EASY ON ROAST BOAR ...
I CAN STOP AVOIDING CONFLICT! I CAN STOP AVOIDING CONFLICT! I CAN STOP ...
41B
YOU'RE NOT HAVING IT! THIS SCROLL BELONGS TO CAESAR!
GRRR
AND YOU MUST RENDER UNTO CAESAR THE THINGS THAT ARE CAESAR'S!
41C

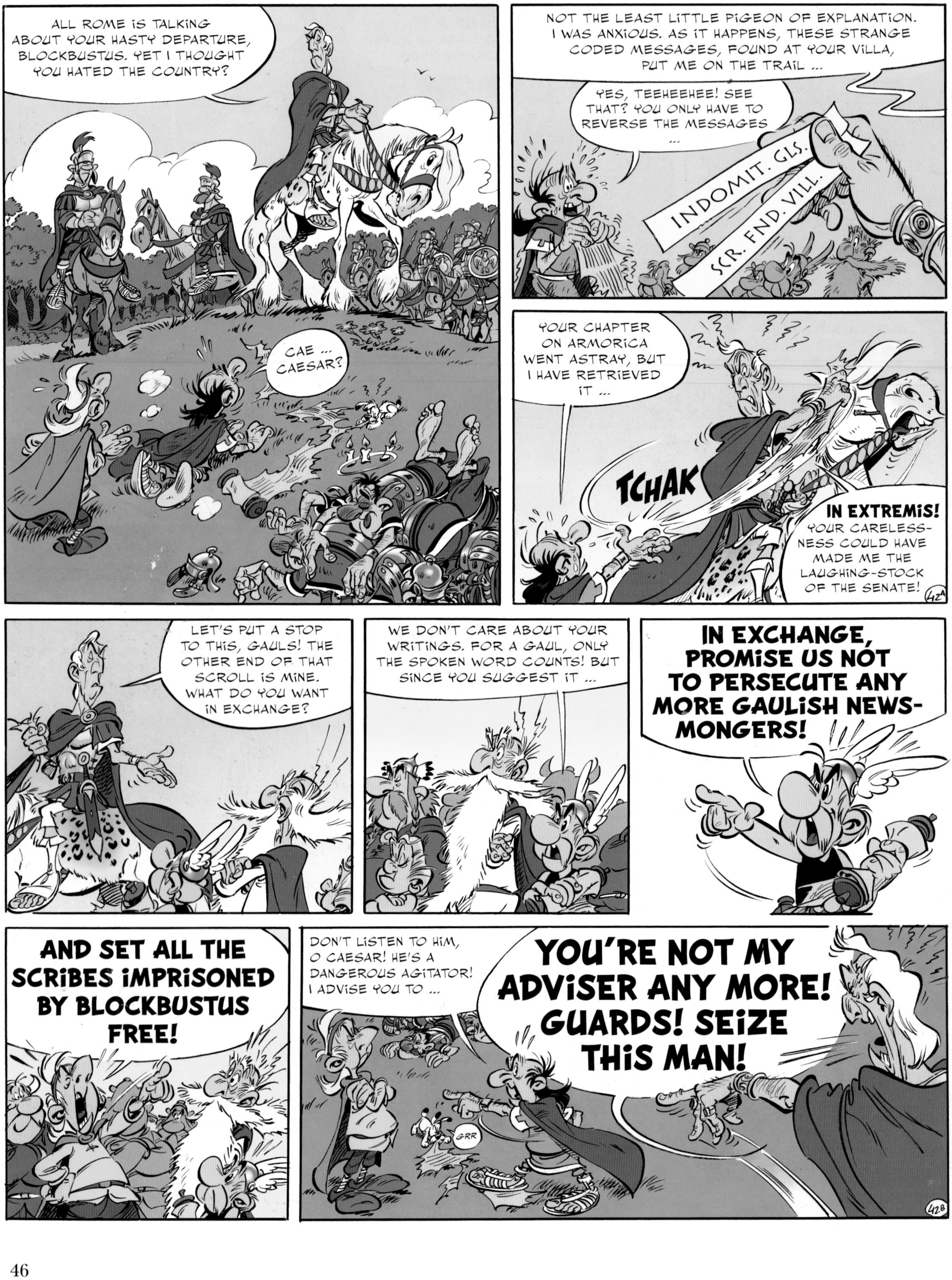
ALL ROME IS TALKING ABOUT YOUR HASTY DEPARTURE, BLOCKBUSTUS. YET I THOUGHT YOU HATED THE COUNTRY?
CAE ... CAESAR?
NOT THE LEAST LITTLE PIGEON OF EXPLANATION. I WAS ANXIOUS. AS IT HAPPENS, THESE STRANGE CODED MESSAGES, FOUND AT YOUR VILLA, PUT ME ON THE TRAIL ...
YES, TEEHEEHEE! SEE THAT? YOU ONLY HAVE TO REVERSE THE MESSAGES ...
INDOMIT. GLS.
SCR. FND. VILL.
YOUR CHAPTER ON ARMORICA WENT ASTRAY, BUT I HAVE RETRIEVED IT ...
TCHAK
IN EXTREMIS! YOUR CARELESS-NESS COULD HAVE MADE ME THE LAUGHING-STOCK OF THE SENATE!
42A
LET'S PUT A STOP TO THIS, GAULS! THE OTHER END OF THAT SCROLL IS MINE. WHAT DO YOU WANT IN EXCHANGE?
WE DON'T CARE ABOUT YOUR WRITINGS. FOR A GAUL, ONLY THE SPOKEN WORD COUNTS! BUT SINCE YOU SUGGEST IT ...
IN EXCHANGE, PROMISE US NOT TO PERSECUTE ANY MORE GAULISH NEWS-MONGERS!
AND SET ALL THE SCRIBES IMPRISONED BY BLOCKBUSTUS FREE!
DON'T LISTEN TO HIM, O CAESAR! HE'S A DANGEROUS AGITATOR! I ADVISE YOU TO ...
YOU'RE NOT MY ADVISER ANY MORE! GUARDS! SEIZE THIS MAN!
GRR
42B

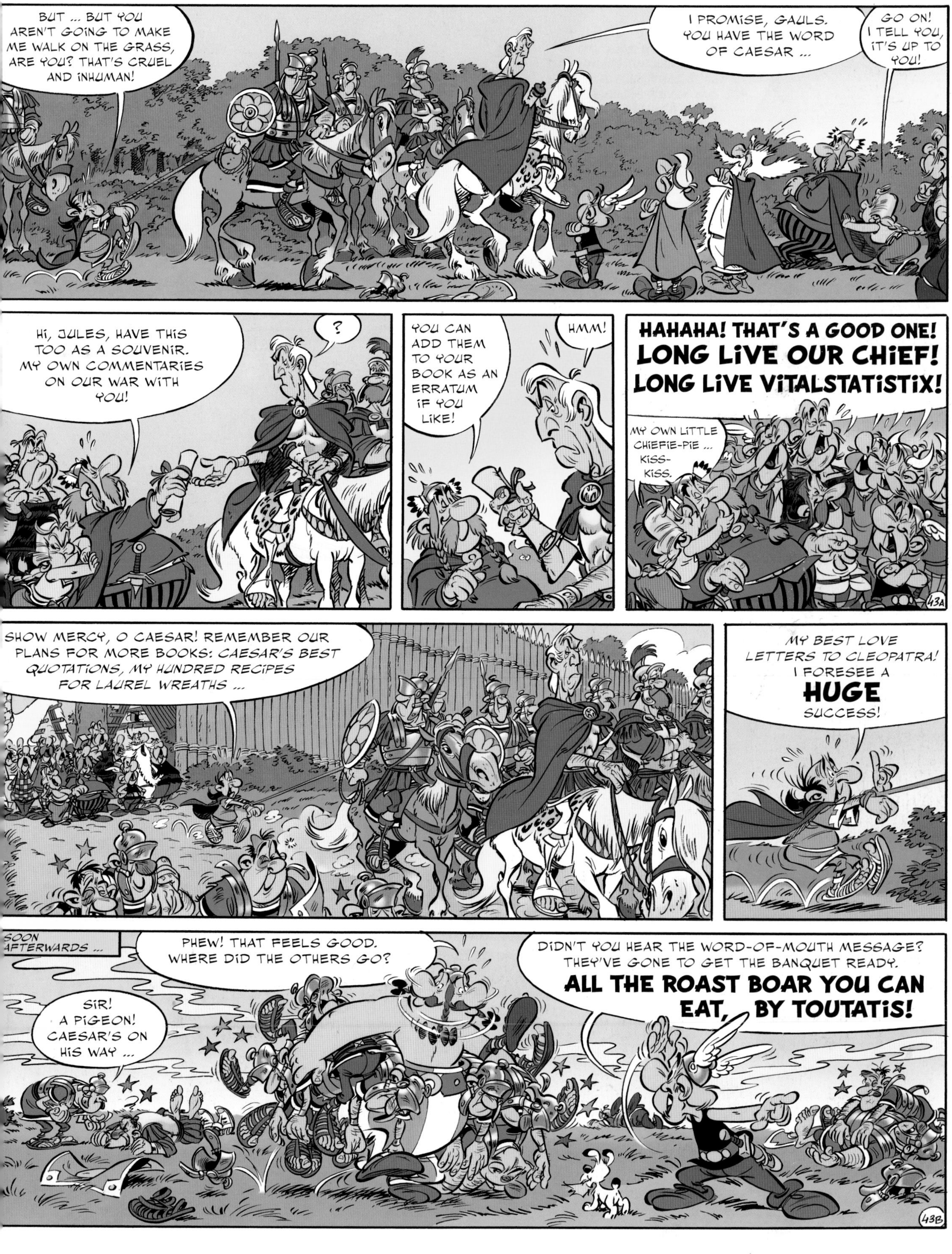

BUT ... BUT YOU AREN'T GOING TO MAKE ME WALK ON THE GRASS, ARE YOU? THAT'S CRUEL AND INHUMAN!
I PROMISE, GAULS. YOU HAVE THE WORD OF CAESAR ...
GO ON! I TELL YOU, IT'S UP TO YOU!
HI, JULES, HAVE THIS TOO AS A SOUVENIR. MY OWN COMMENTARIES ON OUR WAR WITH YOU!
?
YOU CAN ADD THEM TO YOUR BOOK AS AN ERRATUM IF YOU LIKE!
HMM!
HAHAHA! THAT'S A GOOD ONE! LONG LIVE OUR CHIEF! LONG LIVE VITALSTATISTIX!
MY OWN LITTLE CHIEFIE-PIE ... KISS-KISS.
43A
SHOW MERCY, O CAESAR! REMEMBER OUR PLANS FOR MORE BOOKS: CAESAR'S BEST QUOTATIONS, MY HUNDRED RECIPES FOR LAUREL WREATHS ...
MY BEST LOVE LETTERS TO CLEOPATRA! I FORESEE A HUGE SUCCESS!
SOON AFTERWARDS ...
PHEW! THAT FEELS GOOD. WHERE DID THE OTHERS GO?
DIDN'T YOU HEAR THE WORD-OF-MOUTH MESSAGE? THEY'VE GONE TO GET THE BANQUET READY. ALL THE ROAST BOAR YOU CAN EAT, BY TOUTATIS!
SIR! A PIGEON! CAESAR'S ON HIS WAY ...
43B

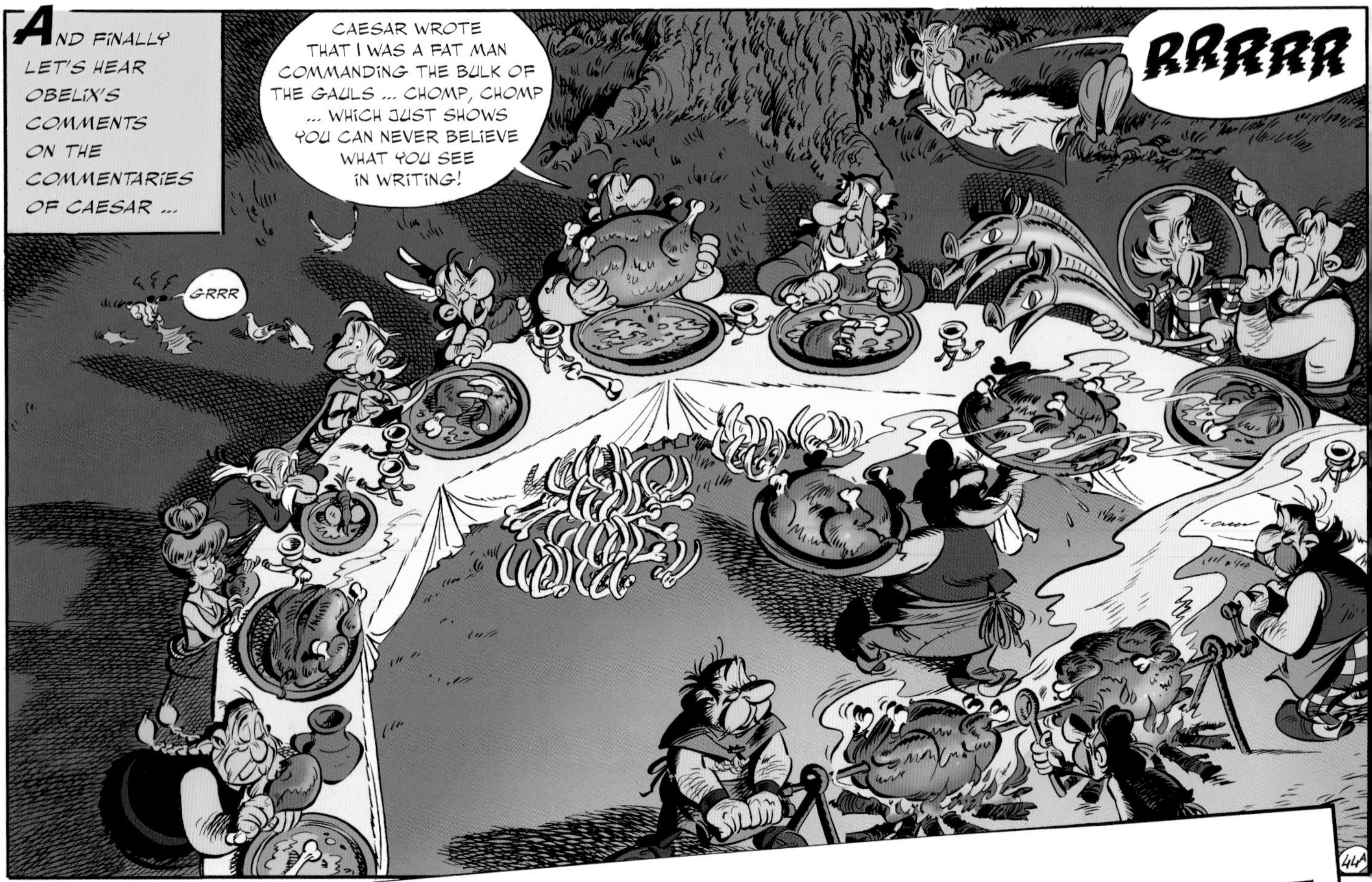
AND FINALLY LET'S HEAR OBELIX'S COMMENTS ON THE COMMENTARIES OF CAESAR ...
CAESAR WROTE THAT I WAS A FAT MAN COMMANDING THE BULK OF THE GAULS ... CHOMP, CHOMP ... WHICH JUST SHOWS YOU CAN NEVER BELIEVE WHAT YOU SEE IN WRITING!
RRRRR
GRRR

Post-Scriptum

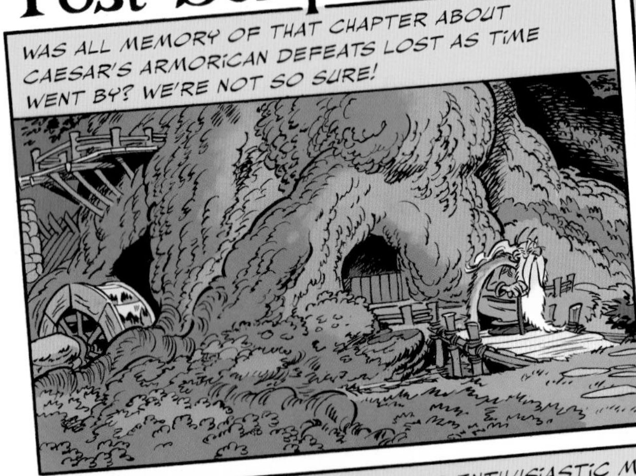
WAS ALL MEMORY OF THAT CHAPTER ABOUT CAESAR'S ARMORICAN DEFEATS LOST AS TIME WENT BY? WE'RE NOT SO SURE!

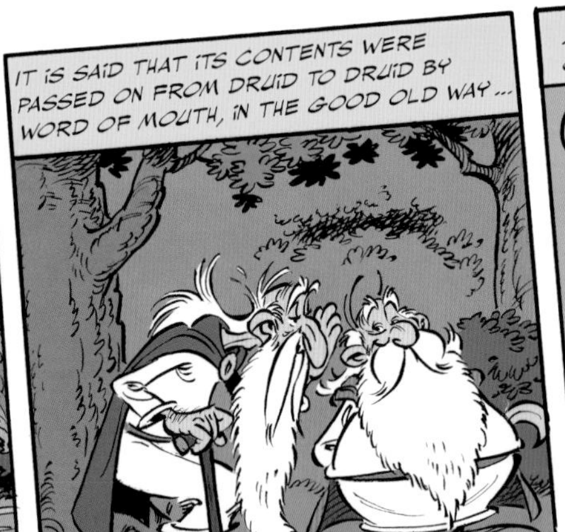
IT IS SAID THAT ITS CONTENTS WERE PASSED ON FROM DRUID TO DRUID BY WORD OF MOUTH, IN THE GOOD OLD WAY ...

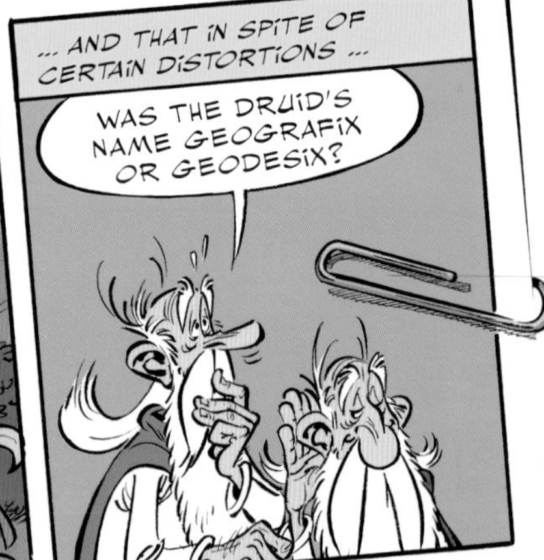
... AND THAT IN SPITE OF CERTAIN DISTORTIONS ...
WAS THE DRUID'S NAME GEOGRAFIX OR GEODESIX?

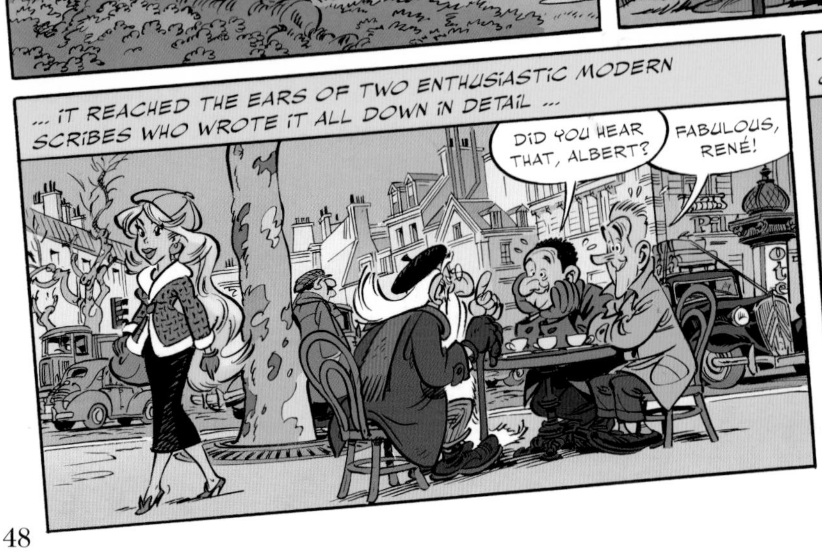
... IT REACHED THE EARS OF TWO ENTHUSIASTIC MODERN SCRIBES WHO WROTE IT ALL DOWN IN DETAIL ...
DID YOU HEAR THAT, ALBERT?
FABULOUS, RENÉ!

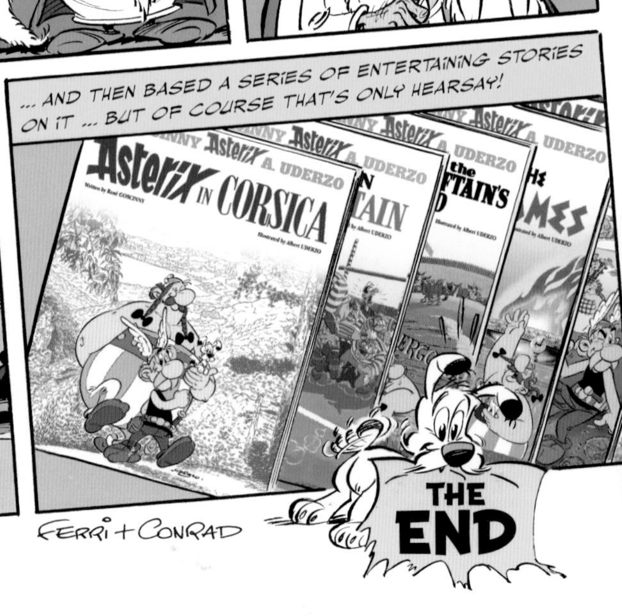
... AND THEN BASED A SERIES OF ENTERTAINING STORIES ON IT ... BUT OF COURSE THAT'S ONLY HEARSAY!
ASTERIX IN CORSICA
A. UDERZO
THE END

FERRI + CONRAD

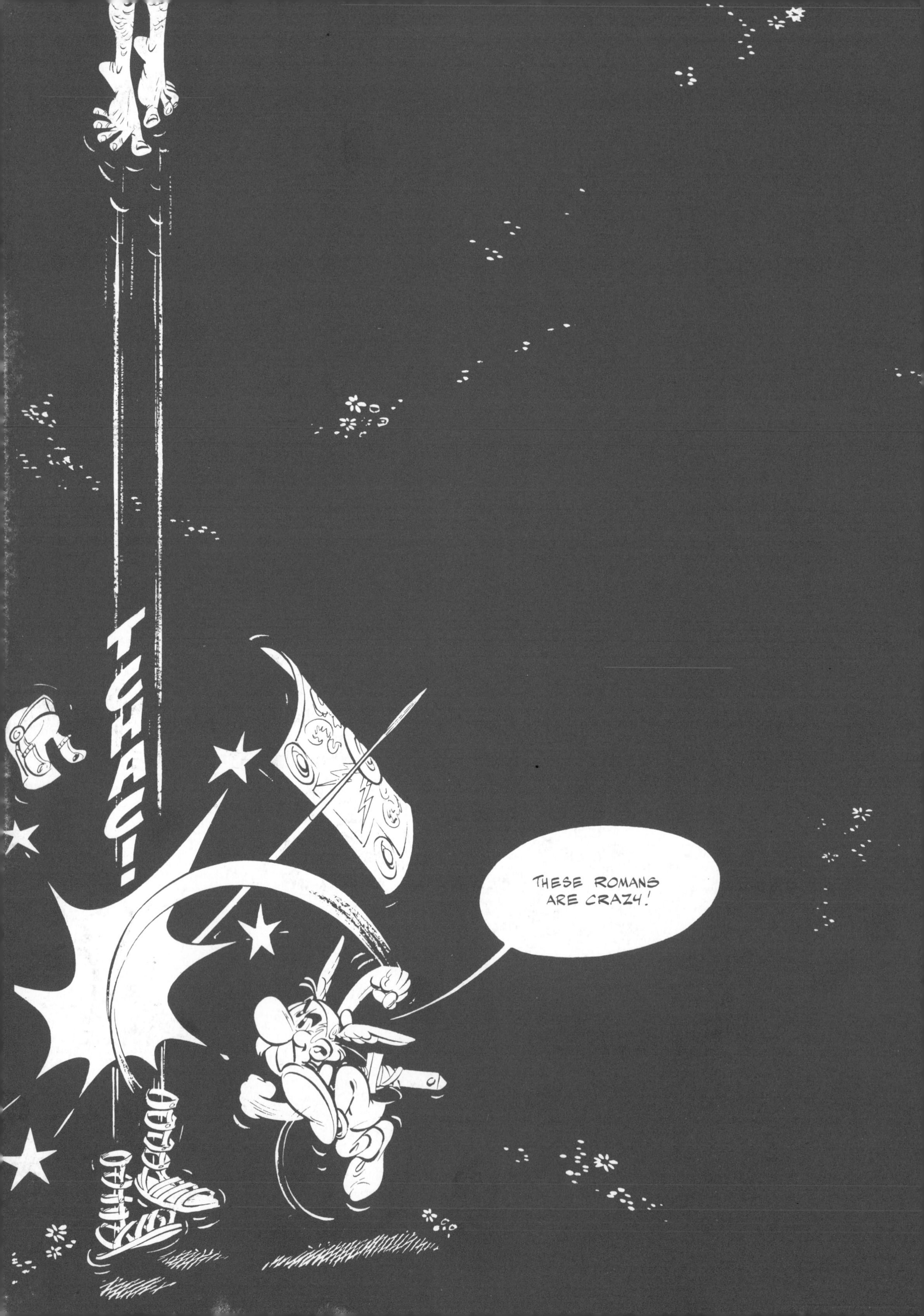
TCHAC!!
THESE ROMANS ARE CRAZY!